NOT AS WE KNEW IT

NOT AS WE KNEW IT

by

F. M. Meredith

NOT AS WE KNEW IT

Edited by Lorna Collins
Cover design by Larry Collins

Print ISBN-13: 9798564552684
eBook ASIN: B08NGLMZJC

ROCKY BLUFF P.D. MYSTERIES

Contents

Dedication

~~ To all those who have experienced loss
due to the COVID 19 virus.
And to all the police officers who
continue to protect us.
And as always, to my dear husband
who has put up with me all these years. ~~

Acknowledgements

- Thanks to Susie Bishop who shared her COVID-19 experience with me.

- Another big thank you to grandson, Officer Gregg Cole, who gave me some great ideas.

- Thanks to fellow Public Safety Writer's Association member, Ron Corbin, who supplied information that inspired one of the crimes in this tale.

- I'm grateful to friends and family members who have a multitude of different theories about the virus.

- Finally, many thanks to Lorna and Larry Collins, wonderful friends who've done so much for me.

Disclaimer

This is what I always tell people when I give talks about the Rocky Bluff P.D. crime series:

"I'm writing fiction. It's my police department so I can do it any way I want."

F. M. Meredith

Chapter 1

Except for thieves stealing packages off front porches, the occasional burglar, and the usual rash of drunk drivers, the holidays had been reasonably crime free. The new year brought a whole new set of problems, including the Coronavirus or COVID-19. This caused a rash of changes for the department, including the wearing of protective masks when dealing with the public.

The governor of California issued guidelines for everyone to follow, but only some of the citizens of Rocky Bluff adhered to the new rules. And though the beach community started out with few cases of the new disease and no deaths, more people had gotten sick, some quarantining themselves at home, and far too many sick enough to go to the hospital.

Restaurants were closed for inside dining, then reopened for a short time, then closed again. Most offered take-out. More people cooked their meals at home. Life had made a radical change, and the change included less criminal activity.

When Detective Doug Milligan's cellphone rang at 11:30 p.m., a sinking feeling in his gut warned him the unusual peace was about to end.

The ID on the phone identified Sergeant Abel Navarro as the caller.

"What's going on, Navarro?" Abel and Doug had been rookies on the Rocky Bluff P.D. at the same time, and good friends ever since.

"Sorry to call you so late on a Saturday night, but we've got a distraught individual who isn't willing to wait until morning to speak with a detective."

"What's the problem?"

"A newcomer to the area, Anthony Portman, lives in one of the new condos at the beach. Says his wife is missing. Fears she's been in an accident or worse."

"Do we know anything about the Portmans?"

"No, he says they've only been here about a month."

"Give me the address and let him know I'll be there in about twenty-minutes."

~~~

No one in Rocky Bluff had wanted the condos to be built except the council members who'd approved them and the contractor. The low-income cottages on the beachfront they replaced for the most part were run-down or trashed. After their demolition, the residents of the town watched the three-story condos being constructed. For many, their ocean view disappeared.

Everyone still had easy access to the beach because a large parking lot remained with a wide pathway leading to the sand. However, those with homes on the lower levels of the town could no longer view the changing blues of the sea.

In Doug's opinion, the biggest fear shared by those living here was that the beach might become popular to outsiders and be overrun by tourists, like Avila and Pismo, with crowded streets, driveways blocked by vehicles, house prices skyrocketing along with property taxes.

As was often the case, at this time of night, a thick fog had rolled in from the sea. Driving was difficult, and Doug had to go slowly to see the numbers on the new homes.

Portman's was the last of twelve condos. All of them had more-or-less the same façade and floor plan, though residents had begun to individualize the front entrances in various ways such as with gnome statues amid a floral garden, an ornate bench set among wine barrels with plants in various stages of growth, and other creative ideas. One had a plain dichondra lawn with a flagstone path.

The street level of each home consisted of a large three-car garage and small front patio. Doug had never been inside any of the units since they'd been completed. He parked his SUV in front of the address he sought with a decorative white fence, put on his face mask, and got out.

A floodlight over the front door lit up a variety of potted plants including some miniature fruit trees.

Before Doug entered the recessed porch, the blue door opened. He displayed his official ID. "I'm Detective Milligan."

A tall man, taller than Doug, and on the chunky side, waved a hand. "Anthony Portman. Detective, thank God you came. I'm beside myself with worry. You have to find Geneva. We've been together for over twenty years." He wore no face covering. He stroked a neat, gray Vandyke beard. Light reflected off his bald head.

"Yes, sir, I'll do my best."

Portman held the door open wide, stepped back, and motioned for Doug to enter.

The area was little more than a foyer with a flight of polished oak stairs leading to the next floor. A large-leafed plant in a barrel stood by the floor-length window. A variety of jackets, sweaters, and hats hung on an old-fashioned coat tree. A white wicker chair sat beside a small table. Doug guessed there was probably a large storage space under the staircase.

"My wife chose this place. She's always wanted to live by the ocean. We lived in Ventura but couldn't afford any of the homes near the beach. She found this condo and pleaded with me to buy it. It was the last one for sale." Portman hung onto the bannister and huffed and puffed as he led the way. A pair of tailored dark-gray trousers covered his substantial backside. "I could have done without all the stairs to reach the living quarters."

The second, and main, floor contained a large living room, a dining area, and a modern kitchen with a balcony, which most likely provided a view of the ocean. Though with the thick fog, nothing could be seen tonight.

Another flight of stairs probably led up to the bedrooms. Doug noticed several doors to the side, maybe a bathroom, laundry, and perhaps pantry.

Portman rubbed his bald head. "I called the CHP to see if Geneva'd had an accident, but they didn't have a report of anything to do with a red Corvette. I don't know what to do."

He seemed understandably upset.

"Start by telling me about your wife. Geneva is her name?"

"Yes, my Geneva. Of course, I'll be happy to tell you all about her. Take a seat, please."

Doug glanced around. In the living room area, a large brown leather sectional, piled high with several orange, yellow, and white pillows, and a matching recliner all faced a huge TV. "Why don't we sit at the table?" He pointed to the white table and matching chairs. It seemed a better place to conduct an interview.

"Oh, yes, of course. Can I give you something to drink, coffee maybe?" Portman glanced around as though he wasn't used to being the host.

"No, I'm fine. Please, sit, and tell me when you last saw your wife."

"Would you mind taking off your mask? I'm a bit hard of hearing and I'm having difficulty understanding you."

Doug complied. It was much easier to breathe without it. He stuck it in his pocket and repeated his question.

"Right after we had lunch. She said she was going shopping, and she'd bring back dinner." He ran his finger around the neck of his white tailored but rumpled shirt.

"Did she tell you where she planned to shop? Here in town or maybe Santa Barbara?"

Portman swallowed hard and shrugged. "She may have, but I'm not good about listening. Geneva is a talker, and like I said, I don't hear so good. I confess I don't pay attention like I should." A tear slid down one puffy cheek.

"Did she drive herself?"

"Yes. Geneva loves her brand-new Corvette. She chose the color herself, bright red."

Doug asked for the license number.

Portman rattled if off without hesitation.

Doug wrote it down. "Do you have a recent photo of her? I'll make copies and return it to you."

The photo he was given looked like a vacation picture, the background a beach scene. A woman probably in her late fifties or early sixties, Geneva Portman had taken good care of herself. The above-the-knee shorts and tank top revealed a body that had regularly exercise. Blonde hair in a fashionable-style surrounded a smiling, pleasant face, which may have had a bit of surgical help.

"I told you, Geneva loves the ocean. Every vacation we took had to be near a beach."

"I have to ask. Do you or your wife have any enemies?"

Portman blinked several times and frowned. "If we do, I don't know who they are. Heck, we haven't even made any friends since we moved in, much less enemies."

"What about where you came from? Ventura, didn't you say?"

Portman nodded. "My boss wasn't happy I chose to retire now, but I think it's because he likes me."

"Is there any reason why your wife might have left on her own?"

This struck a nerve. Portman raised his voice a few notches. "Absolutely not. I told you. She was the one who wanted to move here. We plan on living here for the rest of our lives." He hefted himself out of his chair and moved to the French doors leading to the patio. "This morning, she sat out there and drank her morning coffee staring at the ocean. She thanked me for making her dream come true."

After promising to do everything in his power to locate the missing woman, Doug headed back to the station. The fog had grown even thicker, causing him to drive more slowly. He filed his report, put out a BOLO, "Be on the Lookout," for the missing woman, Geneva Portman, and her car, included her photo and description and license number of the Corvette. No sooner had he finished than Abel Navarro called him again.

"We've had a call from the fire department about a suspicious house fire on Dahlia. You might want to drop by there on your way home."

~ ~ ~

Despite the fog, flames and smoke were visible from the police station. Doug parked as close as he could get to the address Abel had given him. He had to walk past two police cars and two fire trucks before he could see what little remained of the fully engulfed two-story wood-framed house. Some of the neighbors stood on their front lawns watching firemen aiming their hoses on the flames.

Doug found the fire captain, Greg Santori, standing by, directing his men. "Are all the residents out of the house?"

Santori, a big man dressed in turn-out gear, glanced toward Doug. His tanned face grimaced. "Neighbors say the family included a man, his wife, and three kids. We probably won't know if anyone was in there until tomorrow sometime." He gave one of his men some directions.

"Any idea how this started?"

"Several of the neighbors say they were wakened by an explosion." Santori shook his head. "We'll have no idea what caused it until we can get in there."

"Thanks. I'll be back." So much for a day of rest. Doug's Sunday would be busy.

Chapter 2

Since the governor had ordered churches to be closed along with non-essential businesses, St. Mark's Catholic Church services were being shown on the Internet. Ryan Strickland's wife, Barbara, insisted the whole family watch together. Barbara's two youngest sons from her first marriage, Philip and Daryl, had grudgingly slouched onto one of the couches. Though her eldest son, Tony, was home from college because of the virus, he'd pleaded he had a paper to write. College classes were being held online.

Angel, Ryan and Barbara's daughter, sat on the carpet happily playing with her toys. Because Angel had Down syndrome, she was classified as more susceptible to the virus, and Barbara insisted the entire family be extra vigilant about washing their hands frequently and always wearing masks when away from home. And she limited their times away to only essential errands.

Before Ryan could sit down next to his wife, his cellphone rang. He glanced at it. "The station."

Barbara sighed and shook her head, making her dark curls bob around her face, though at the moment not such a happy face.

He listened intently. "I'll be there right away." He patted Barbara's shoulder. "Sorry, honey. I have to go in."

"Be sure to wear your mask." Barbara reminded him as she always did when he had to leave the house.

"Wish someone needed me." Philip frowned. "It's dumb for all of us to be watching like this. We could do it in our own rooms."

Ryan knew if Philip had been allowed to watch the church service in his room, he wouldn't have. Barbara knew her sons well.

Ryan still couldn't help but be amazed by how happy he was. His life had changed so much since he'd married Barbara. He'd been assigned to help her when her husband was killed in the line of duty, and his admiration for her strength had changed into love. Certainly not the type of woman he'd been attracted to previously, there was something about the plump, curly-haired, talkative widow and strong woman that captivated him. Everyone had been surprised, including Ryan, when she agreed to marry him.

An even bigger surprise came when Barbara became pregnant. The fact that Angel had Down syndrome didn't faze Ryan. To him, Angel was the most beautiful and precious child in the world.

The last thing Ryan heard as he headed to the bedroom to change into his uniform was Barbara talking to her sons. "It doesn't seem like church unless we all worship together."

~~~

At the Milligan household, while Doug ate a quick breakfast before heading back to the station, his family ate more leisurely, though his wife, Stacey, informed him she and the kids planned to attend church services.

"Church? I thought all the churches were supposed to be closed down."

Stacey, who had the day off, said, "They are, but Reverend Cookmeyer is trying something different. We're all meeting in the parking lot and remaining in our cars.

Cookmeyer will be preaching from a platform on the lawn and using a sound system."

Stacey's short hair made her appear far younger than she was. Doug had been enamored of her from the first. He'd met her when she assisted him in solving a double murder case. Though she'd vowed not to date fellow police officers, Doug had persisted until she agreed to see him socially and finally to marriage.

"They won't let us have Sunday School either, but I can wave out the car window to all my friends." Stacey's son, Davey, seemed enthusiastic about the outing.

Doug thought about his wife and the two kids and Beth's friend, Kayla, all crammed in her VW bug. Davey, the youngest was Stacey's from her first marriage, and Beth was his. "How about trading cars? You'll be a lot more comfortable in the SUV."

"Great idea, Dad." His daughter, Beth, hadn't let the coronavirus stop her from wearing unusual outfits, today a purple skirt with an irregular hemline, and a top created with two colorful scarfs wound strategically over her chest and tied in back. Her dyed blonde hair had several colorful streaks: red, blue, turquoise, and orange."

Kayla Duval, the mayor's daughter, was Beth's best friend and the only one Doug and Stacey let her have personal contact with. With school closed, the students kept their cellphones and iPads busy with video chats, FaceTime, and other forms of communication. When Beth asked if Kayla could stay with them, Doug and Stacey had agreed as did her father, since all the adults had to work.

Of course, schoolwork was done online, too. Beth had been a big help getting Davey set up on his new iPad and helped him whenever he got stuck.

"We're all going to my parents' for dinner after the service. If you can get away on your lunch break, stop by.

Otherwise, I'll bring a plate home for you." Stacey's mother and father insisted that the virus wasn't going to keep them from seeing their family. Besides, since Davey was doing his schoolwork online, he might as well stay with his grandparents for a couple of days as he'd done before the virus struck.

Though Stacey had argued that her parents' age put them in the vulnerable category, and since Beth had to stay home, too, she could babysit. Before Beth could complain, Clare Osborne argued that depriving her of spending time with her grandson would cause her and her husband undue heartache.

Stacey handed Doug her keys. "What's going on?"

"Missing woman and a suspicious house fire. Got to get going. I'll give you the details when I come home."

~~~

As Doug drove to work, he called his partner, Felix Zachary. The two detectives worked together and handled all the major crimes. Besides their police chief, Zachary was the only other African American in the department. He and Doug made a good team. They'd both been on the department nearly the same amount of time and had similar work ethics. Like Doug, Zachary was married and had one daughter, though his daughter, Ruby, was a toddler.

"Gonna need your help today, Felix."

"What's going on?"

Doug could hear Felix's wife, Wendy, talking in the background.

"Suspicious house fire and a missing woman. Sounds like your wife is not happy."

"We're having our folks over for dinner today. They're not going to let the virus keep them from seeing their granddaughter. Wendy can handle it."

From what Doug could hear coming from the background Wendy didn't sound like she agreed with her husband. "Okay, see you in a bit."

The fog had rolled in again, but not as thick as yesterday, and with it, the salty scent of the ocean.

~~~

Once Doug arrived at the station, he checked in with Sergeant Ryan Strickland, another veteran from the time they'd both been young cops.

Ryan, tall and dark-haired, looked handsome and spiffy in his uniform, as always. "I've been making sure everyone out in the field knows about the missing woman. Do you think it's foul play, or something else?"

"At this point, I have no idea. Perhaps she had an accident in her brand-new car. If so, we should be hearing soon."

"I'm surprised you came in for that."

"I didn't. I want to check on the house fire. Once Zachary arrives, we're going to go talk to the fire captain. He's expecting me."

"Something suspicious about it?"

"Maybe, but I'm more interested in whether or not the occupants were still in there."

Before he could say more, Felix Zachary strode in wearing what looked like brand-new slacks and his usual sport jacket over a dark blue polo shirt. As always, with his muscular stature and piercing eyes, he appeared sharp and menacing at the same time.

After they greeted each other, Doug said, "Captain Santori is waiting for us at the fire scene." He paused. "And by the way, we either need to go in your car or check out one of the unmarkeds. I've had to drive my wife's VW bug today."

The detectives walked toward the back exit.

Felix laughed. "I'd never be able to fold myself up to be able to get in the VW. What's the matter, having trouble with your van?"

"No. Stacey and the kids are going to church in it."

Felix halted. "Church? I thought the governor said churches had to be closed."

"The building is closed, but they're having services in the parking lot."

He shrugged and raised his thick eyebrows. "Not a bad idea."

~~~

Captain Santori and another man, both wearing boots and overalls over their clothes, didn't look happy when Doug and Felix approached.

Santori held up palm and shook his head. "We can't let you in any farther. We've found five bodies."

"Did you call the medical examiner?" Doug asked.

"Of course. Someone from Ventura should be arriving soon." He turned to the other man who seemed familiar to Doug. "This is the department's certified arson investigator, Phil Peterson."

Peterson, a small man, with black-framed glasses perched on a long skinny nose, nodded in their direction. They would usually shake hands, but the current safety protocols prohibited it. "Nasty scene, and from what little I've had a chance to see, it looks like arson."

"Anyone know who the deceased are?" Doug asked.

"One of the neighbors said the Barberick family lived here, father, mother and three kids." Santori shook his head. "Only thing I can let you do right now is stand outside the perimeter to take pictures. You'll have to wait for the medical examiner to let you get any closer."

"I'm next in line." Peterson grimaced. "I've seen enough to know that the fire was set, but I have to make a much closer examination to figure out how."

"I was told there was an explosion." Doug stepped over debris to get closer to the destroyed outside walls.

"I have a theory about it, but I won't know for sure until I can examine the scene." Peterson stood with legs and arms spread as though he expected Doug to push past him.

"Don't worry, I'm not going to contaminate the crime scene." Doug pulled out his phone. "I'm calling the chief."

"Why not wait until tomorrow?" Felix asked.

"Not long ago, I got in trouble with her because I didn't let her know about something right away, something not nearly as big as what we've got here."

Doug didn't have to wait long for Chief Taylor to answer. "What's going on, Milligan?"

He explained the situation. "We can't do much yet. I'll take what pictures I can from outside of what's left of the house, and then Zachary and I are going to start questioning the neighbors to see what we can find out about the victims."

"Keep me posted." Surprisingly, she asked no questions and ended the call.

With almost everything closed, Doug doubted he'd interrupted much, unless of course the chief was having a romantic interlude with the mayor. The idea was doubtful. Since the mayor's daughter had come into the picture, according to Stacey who knew much more about such happenings than he did, the romance had nearly come to a halt. Dealing with the problems caused by the virus probably didn't help either.

Besides the strong smell of smoke, burnt wood, and ash, Doug detected the unmistakable scent of cooked flesh. It didn't take long to spot the burnt corpse of what had once been a man and a much smaller body, perhaps an infant, close to the larger remains. From where Doug stood, the partial burned remnants of the house blocked his view of the other victims. He used his cell to take several photos.

"Sad. Come on, Felix, let's see what we can find out about the deceased family from the neighbors."

Chapter 3

His cellphone woke Abel Navarro from a pleasant dream. It was Sunday and surprisingly, both he and his wife, Maria, had the day off.

As soon as he said hello, his brother Mario, began shouting. "I told you that woman would be nothing but trouble. We have to do something and do it fast."

"What are you talking about?" Though Abel asked, he figured it had to do with Ysabel, the woman who had taken care of his mother until she died, and had become close to her father, so close she'd moved in. Something Mario had not been pleased about from the beginning. As far as Abel was concerned, his father deserved to be happy, and he and Ysabel seemed to be having a great time together.

"She won't let anyone visit dad. Who does she think she is? She's turned him into a prisoner."

The phone awakened Maria, and she frowned at Abel. "What's going on?"

"It's Mario. He says Ysabel won't let anyone in to see our father."

"Give me your phone." She held out her hand.

Abel turned the phone over to her.

"Listen to me, Mario. Ysabel is protecting your father's health. He's old, which makes him susceptible to COVID-19. He shouldn't be around anyone who lives outside his home right now."

Abel could hear Mario shouting. "You think you're so smart. Just because you're a nurse doesn't mean you know everything."

Maria kept her voice calm. "I don't know everything, but I do know about this virus. It's worse for the elderly when they get it. We've already had two deaths at the hospital, both around your dad's age. The emergency room is full all the time. What you're hearing on the news and the Internet is right. This is a highly contagious disease that we don't know a whole lot about. I've been working extra shifts, and this is my first day off in two weeks. Be glad someone is looking out for your father's welfare."

"I have my own opinion about what is going on." He disconnected.

Maria sighed loudly. "You know how your brother is. He certainly ruined our sleep. We might as well get up."

A nurse, Maria worked in the emergency room, and when she came home from work she undressed in the garage and threw her clothes in the washer. She took a hot shower using disinfectant soap and donned fresh clothes before she would greet either Abel or their daughter, Lupita. She'd warned Abel if things got much worse, she might not come home at all, but stay at the hospital.

"It's bad out there. People don't realize how easily this disease is passed on. A sneeze or cough can carry the virus in droplets to many others. We're trying to educate everyone to wear masks and really wash their hands thoroughly. I'm so happy Chief Taylor has required everyone in the department to wear masks when in public." Already out of bed, Maria headed for the bathroom.

Though Abel had protested, his wife had cut her long black hair to a more manageable length, though still long enough to put in a bun or ponytail. All the hard work she'd been subjected to lately had resulted in her shapely body becoming a bit leaner. As always, she looked fantastic, though a bit weary.

Abel didn't bother to tell her the dispatchers didn't always wear their masks, and most of the officers didn't bother when they were inside the police station. As far as he knew, everyone was pretty good about wearing them when on patrol, including him when he joined an investigation.

"I hear Lupita. I'll get her and start making breakfast."

With the day care closed because of the virus, four-year-old Lupita was either at home with Abel, or when he worked, with his other brother's wife. They had two kids, and though Maria wasn't thrilled to have Lupita in contact with other children, she'd given Juan's wife, Veronica, detailed instructions about how to protect those in her care.

Lupita met him in the hall, a big grin on her beautiful face. "Hi, Daddy." She resembled Maria in so many ways with her long black hair, today braided in a single plait, and beautiful like her mom.

No matter what might be wrong in the world, a smile from Lupita made the day wonderful for Abel.

~ ~ ~

After Doug and Felix, both wearing their masks, spoke with the neighbors on both sides of the street, the information they'd learned about the victims was about the same from all they'd talked with.

They'd knocked on the door of the house next to the burned house. It had been answered by an older heavyset woman who introduced herself as Mrs. Cardova. "I suspect you've heard about the family next door. From what's going on, I suspect they didn't make it."

Doug put his wallet back in his pocket, "We'd like to find out what we can about your neighbors."

"Would you like to come in?" She opened the door wider.

"That won't be necessary."

"The family more or less kept to themselves. Mr. and Mrs. Barberick. Jim and Lauren. They have three children, Caleb, who I think was ten, Caroline, a couple of years younger and a little one, Mary, who was probably nine-months old. I saw enough of the children to know they were well-behaved. Jim went to work every day, the children attended school and from what I could tell, Lauren spent her time tending to her family and her house."

"Do you know if they had any problems?"

Mrs. Cardova frowned. "Certainly nothing I knew about."

Doug handed her one of his cards. "Thank you, and if you should think of anything else, give me a call."

"I doubt you'll hear from me, I barely knew them despite living next-door."

The detectives went from house to house, but everyone they spoke to thought the Barbericks were a normal, happy family, though no one knew them well.

By the time the detectives returned to the scene of the fire, three technicians from the medical examiners' office had arrived. Wearing white covering from head to toe, they'd managed to wade through the ashes and burned debris and were taking pictures from many angles.

Doug couldn't see much, because the techs were working behind a collapsed wall and a section of the room. He surmised from their actions, the bodies of the mother and the other children were there. He knew they were taking photos.

Doug was itching to get in and take his own photos. He moved close to Peterson, who he could tell was just as anxious as he was. "Any chance I can get in there to take closeups of the bodies before they are taken away?"

"Okay, if you let me lead you in. You'll have to step where I tell you."

"I'll do whatever you want."

"Get some coverings over your shoes so you're ready. I don't think it'll be long now."

Doug got booties out of the trunk of the unmarked car they'd driven and put them on. If he had the opportunity to examine the remains of the house itself, he'd have suited up appropriately, but that wasn't going to be allowed until Peterson had finished with his job. Doug didn't expect that to happen anytime soon, if at all.

The guys from the medical examiners' office knew Doug wanted photos before they removed the bodies, and it wasn't long before they waved at him. One of the men called out, "Come get your pictures now. We're ready to load up these remains."

Peterson motioned to Doug. "Follow me now." The man moved painfully slow, stopping to peer at one thing and then another, snapping photos as he went.

Doug stepped as carefully as he could exactly in Peterson's footprints. Taking advantage of the times his leader paused, Doug took his own pictures. First a close-up of the father and baby, other objects that interested the arson investigator, and when they approached the other three bodies, the men from the M.E.'s office stepped back a couple of feet, allowing Doug and Peterson full view of the other three corpses.

The fire had been intense and the burnt remains barely resembled a mother and two children. Doug took many photos, from one angle and then another. He wasn't unhappy when the head medical examiner said, "We need to take care of these remains now."

There was no point in arguing.

Peterson touched Doug's arm. "Follow me out."

Before Doug turned to leave, he spoke to the techs from the ME's office. "Give me a call as soon as you have information about the deceased."

"We will, but it won't be soon."

Doug thanked them. He focused on Peterson. The arson investigator knelt down examining something.

Doug called out to him. "What do you see?"

"At this point, I'm saying definitely arson. My guess, fire ignited natural gas, hence the explosion the neighbors reported. It'll take a while to come up with what exactly happened here."

"You thinking this is a homicide case?" Definitely Doug's thought at this point.

Peterson's expression remained grim. "We won't know until we hear the results of the autopsy reports, but my best guess is yes."

"The way the bodies are positioned, I wonder if the father killed his wife and the two children."

"Could be, and my guess is he didn't expect the explosion, or at least not so soon. If he was guilty, I suspect he thought he'd be out before the explosion. We'll have some answers later."

There wasn't anything more Doug and Felix could do at the fire scene. They certainly had heard nothing from the neighbors to indicate the family had troubles. They'd have to do more digging. Time to find out who the relatives were and deliver the bad news. Perhaps one of them would know more about what was going on with the Barberick family.

Turning to Captain Santori, who'd remained at the perimeter of the ruins of the house, Doug said, "We'd like to know what else Peterson learns as soon as possible."

Santori nodded. "Of course."

Zachary followed Doug back to their car. "What now?"

"First, we'll have to find out who the closest relatives are and let them know what happened. While we're at it, we can ask some questions."

Zachary climbed into the driver's seat. "Are we going to do anything about the missing woman today?"

The fog had lifted some, making the driving easier.

Doug slid into the passenger seat. "Let's give the missing woman's husband a call and find out if he's heard anything from her. We'll check if anyone has spotted her car. If not, we'll see what the chief thinks about Strickland putting information about her on TV."

Besides being a sergeant, Strickland also was the public information officer. Doug knew it was a job he loved. For a while, the new chief had handled the duty of keeping the public informed, but not long before, she'd handed responsibility back to Strickland.

"Mrs. Portman hasn't been missing all that long." Zachary started the car.

"I know, but I have a weird feeling about her disappearance."

Zachary stared at Doug. "Are you thinking maybe the husband had something to do with this?"

"Not yet, but something isn't adding up. If the woman had an accident in that fancy new car of hers, surely we'd have heard by now."

Chapter 4

Remarkably, as she always did, Stacey's mother, Clara Osborne, managed to have dinner on the table only a few minutes after the whole family walked in the door. She'd scooped her white hair into a bun and smiled as she worked. She'd tied an apron around her waist to protect what she referred to as her "Sunday go to meeting" dress.

The menu consisted of chicken alfredo and small bowl of noodles with sauce minus the meat for Beth, a big vegetable salad, and garlic bread.

Stacey couldn't help glancing at her watch after her father said the blessing. She doubted Doug would have the chance to stop by to eat. "Looks great, Mom. Don't know how you do it."

"Planning and a lot of preparation before we leave for church. What did you think about the new arrangement?" Clara passed the bread.

Clyde, Stacey's father, scooped a big helping of the Alfredo onto his plate. "Foolishness if you ask me. Absolutely no reason we can't meet in church as always. We could comply with the separation rules. Your mom and I and many others would be willing to sanitize everything before and after. The governor is going too far with all this silly nonsense. He's getting a thrill out of his power plays."

Davey pouted. "I miss Sunday School and real school. Doing school on my tablet is dumb. I want to see my friends in person."

"The new rules are to keep all of us from getting sick. It'll be over soon, I hope." Beth, a vegetarian, offered the bowl of the meatless noodles to Kayla. Stacey's mom always made sure to have plenty of food Beth could eat.

"No, thanks. I'm going to have the one with chicken. Looks and smells delicious." Kayla, Beth's friend, with her halo of blonde curls had topped them with a silver butterfly barrette.

"It's not fair. I can't see any of my friends, but Beth gets to have Kayla." Davey's complaint didn't keep him from filling his plate and eating.

"You get to be with us, Davey. Not many kids can hang out with their grandparents right now." Clyde reached over and rumpled Davey's hair. "We'll keep you busy."

Davey gave up his arguing and concentrated on his food.

Beth nudged Kayla. "I'm so happy your dad is letting you stay with us."

"Me too. Plus, I get to eat all this great food. You'll have to give me the recipe for this Alfredo, Mrs. Osborne. My dad would love it."

"Tell you what. Whenever you girls want, come over and I'll give you cooking lessons." Clara kept the various dishes circulating around the table while conversation continued.

"Awesome." Kayla grinned

Stacey wondered if Beth felt the same way, but she didn't comment. Her phone buzzed, Doug calling. "Sorry, but I need to take this." Stacey scooted her chair back and moved into the semi-privacy of the living room.

"Hey, you're missing out on a great dinner."

"I'm not going to make it there, and you don't need to bring anything home. Felix's wife just delivered a couple of plates for us from the dinner she made for her family."

"How nice. Did she come in wearing a mask and gloves?"

"Nope, she called Felix when she got here, and he went out to her car to get the food."

"What a weird world we're living in today." Stacey felt bad. She wouldn't get to see Doug. "What's going on that's keeping you at work?"

"Bodies turned up in the house fire. A whole family."

"And I'm guessing it might be murder."

"Won't know until we get the medical examiner's report, but it was definitely an arson fire. Soon as we eat, Felix and I are going to deliver the sad news to relatives. We're also working on the missing woman case. Not sure how much longer I'll be. Depends upon what we can turn up."

"I guess I'll see you when you get home. Love you."

"Love you back."

When Stacey returned to the table, Kayla leaned toward Beth. "Your dad's like mine. You never know what he might have to do. Gotten worse since this stupid virus. Gets calls all the time. People expect him to do the impossible. Still has to meet with the city council despite all the new rules."

Clyde made a snorting noise. "Whole world has gone crazy."

"Dad have a new case?" Beth asked.

"A couple. Arson fire and a missing person." Stacey concentrated on her food, but the questions began.

From Beth: "Who's missing?"

Almost before she finished, Davey said, "Who set the fire? What burned down?"

Clara shook her head. "Not now, please. Let's finish dinner. I've got some strawberries from Oxnard, and I made an angel food cake."

"What about whipped cream?"

"Plenty of whipped cream."

Davey's face exploded into a huge smile

~~~

When he and Felix returned to the station, Doug learned Lauren Barberick's father had called. He'd heard about the fire and wanted to know if there were any survivors. He left his phone number and address.

Before heading out on their hard task of delivering the bad news to the relatives of the dead family, Doug called the chief. He brought her up to date on what was going on. "I'd like permission to have Strickland put out information on the TV news about our missing woman. We know so little about her. Maybe if the word gets out, someone might have some information."

She agreed.

Next stop, delivering the devastating information about the dead family.

~~~

Doug and Felix, masks on, stood on the front porch of the address they'd been given for the parents of Lauren Barberick, Mr. and Mrs. James. Located only a few blocks from what had once been the home of their daughter, son-in-law, and grandchildren, Doug knew this was not going to be easy.

When the door opened, Doug could tell by the sad expressions on the two middle-aged parents they already suspected the news he and Felix would bring them. Doug displayed his identification and introduced himself and Felix. "May we come in?"

"Of course." Both of the Jameses stepped aside.

The detectives entered a large living room with two light brown sectionals facing a large-screen TV. "It would be best if you sat down." Doug always encouraged the recipients of bad news to sit. He'd had people collapse and others faint when he'd had to tell them of the death of a relative.

Mr. and Mrs. James sat side-by-side, clutching one another's hands. Tears already streamed down Mrs. James's cheeks.

Doug spoke softly. "There is no easy way to say this. Your daughter, her husband, and three children perished in their house fire."

Mrs. James cried out before burying her head against her husband's shoulder.

Mr. James wiped his eyes and cleared his throat. "Any idea how the fire started?"

Felix reached out and patted Mr. James on the shoulder. "We don't know anything conclusive at this time."

"When will be able to bury our daughter and our grandkids?"

"It may be a while. Right now, they are at the medical examiner's office. When it is possible, I'll let you know." Doug hoped they wouldn't ask any more questions. It was too early to discuss the fact that someone started the fire.

The furrows in Mr. James's forehead deepened. "I don't understand. Why are they at the medical examiner's office? Is something else going on we should know about?"

"Mr. James, this is standard procedure in a situation like this," Felix said.

Doug could tell by the expression on Mr. James's face that the man suspected there was more about his family's death. "What aren't you telling us?"

"Believe me, we don't know anything more than what we've said." *Nothing conclusive anyway, though he had many suspicions.*

"Did my son-in-law have something to do with this?" Mr. James's voice had a note of anger in it.

"Why would you ask?" Felix stood directly in front of the man.

"Something wasn't right with their marriage. Our daughter never said anything, but I could tell by how she acted, something had changed."

Mrs. James clutched her husband's arm. "We don't know anything. He's merely guessing."

Mr. James turned to his wife. "He wasn't happy about having so many kids. You know that. He said it enough times. Our Lauren was always worn out. He expected their house to be spotless all the time. Not an easy task with a houseful of kids. And especially now, when they couldn't go to school or outside to play with their friends."

"Did your daughter have any best friends who might be willing to talk to us?"

Mrs. James lowered her head.

Her husband jutted out his chin. "No. Jim didn't allow her to have any friends. He was mean to her and overbearing."

After biting her lip, Mrs. James said, "She did call her friend Wanda when Jim was working."

Felix pulled his notebook from his pocket. "Do you have Wanda's phone number?"

"No, but her last name is Johnson."

Doug wasn't sure how long it might take them to find the friend. Johnson was a common name. "Any idea where she lives?"

Mr. James raised an eyebrow. "My wife's right. Our daughter and Wanda were best friends all through school. She's still here in Rocky Bluff as far as I know."

Felix continued taking notes. "Is she married?"

Mrs. James nodded. "Our daughter Lauren was Wanda's maid of honor when she got married. Her husband's name was Harold. But I think they have since divorced."

At least we have something to go on. Doug handed his card to Mr. James. "If you think of anything else, please call."

"Will you let us know when we can have a funeral for our daughter and grandkids?" Tears filled the man's eyes.

"Yes, sir. But it may be a while."

Mr. and Mrs. James clutched each other in a tight embrace. Mrs. James sobbed against her husband's shoulder.

Doug and Felix let themselves out the door.

Chapter 5

The doorbell rang right when Maria put the sizzling pan of beef fajitas on the table. "Who on earth could that be?"

Abel didn't have any idea but shoved his chair back and headed into the front room. Before he could reach the door, someone pounded on it.

"Open up, Abel." It was his brother, Mario, still sounding angry.

Abel let Mario in. "What's the problem? We're in the kitchen getting ready to eat."

"Same thing I talked about on the phone. That witch won't let me see our dad." Elbows out, he brushed by Abel.

When he entered the kitchen, Maria held a hand up to block him. "Stop right there. You're not coming any closer without a mask." She pointed to a box of masks on the counter.

"I should have known you'd be a stickler for masks." He put one on and plopped into an empty hair. He stared at the fajitas, the big pan of refried beans, and the container of flour tortillas. "That sure looks good."

"I'll send a plate home with you." Maria sat down and dished up a small amount of beans and fajitas, along with a tortilla for Lupita. "It's hot, honey. Blow on it."

"Why are you here?" Abel stared at Mario. "If Ysabel has made up her mind to keep Dad away from any contamination, isn't it a good thing?"

"He's my father, and I have a right to see him." Mario put his meaty hands on the table. The eldest of the three brothers, he was also the biggest, with broad shoulders, a big chest straining his yellow T-shirt that advertised his construction company, and a bit of a belly that hung over his worn jeans. However, like the others, he had plenty of black hair. He kept his neatly shorn.

Maria filled a plate for Abel. "Ysabel's doing exactly what she should to protect your father. You ought to be glad. His age makes him vulnerable to this virus. We've hospitalized several patients in his age group who've contacted this illness. Most are extremely sick."

"But I'm his son." Mario reached a meaty finger toward the fajitas. "His first born."

Maria blocked it with a napkin over her hand. "The problem is you come in contact with all sorts of people while you're working, right? And I know you don't wear a mask."

"Well, yeah. I'm building houses and have a big crew. Can't breathe with one of these damn masks on."

"You could be carrying the virus without knowing it. You don't want to make your father sick, do you?" Maria stood. "I'll fix you a plate."

"Don't bother, if I took a plate home my wife would be mad. She's making chicken mole." He took one last look at the fajitas and stood. "I knew I wouldn't get any sympathy here. Don't know why I came. I was hoping the two of you would listen to reason." He stomped through the house and slammed the front door.

Lupita called after him, "Bye-bye, Uncle Mario."

"He's the one who won't listen to reason. Let's eat." Abel would like to visit his father, too, but he knew Maria was right. After all, like Mario, he came in contact with all sorts of folks every single day. Sometimes he wore a mask, and sometimes he didn't.

~~~

Gordon Butler and his wife had changed shifts again, Gordon on nights and Lizette days. The reason wasn't making Gordon happy. Sunday was their one day off together and Lizette had made his favorite Filipino dishes: *lumpia,* somewhat like spring rolls with a ground beef filling and deep fried, *pancit,* rice noodles with vegetables and a flavorful sauce.

After he'd eaten his fill, he pushed his chair back. "Delicious as always."

"I can tell you're not happy about something, Gordon. Talk to me."

Lizette and Gordon could still be considered newlyweds. Gordon still thanked God for bringing the beautiful Lizette into his life. The blend of her Filipino, Native American, and Anglo heritage gave her an exotic appearance. She wore her dark, nearly black hair in short bob. It framed her heart-shaped face, with big up-turned eyes, and smooth honey-colored skin.

Gordon had given up on having a happy marriage when Lizette first came on the job. She hadn't been attracted to him at first, but her feelings had soon changed.

In many ways, his whole life had improved. Not only did he have Lizette as a life partner, but his co-workers treated him with far more respect than they had in the past.

What bothered him now was the new assignment given Lizette by Chief Taylor. "If you must know. I don't understand why the chief wants you to be the training officer for this new recruit. You haven't been on the job very long."

Lizette grinned. "I suppose you think she should have used you again."

"I would have been a better choice."

"I think she wants me to have the experience. Maybe it's a test of some sort."

"Has she told you anything about this guy?"

"No, but don't stress yourself over it. If I have any problems, I'll be sure to ask your opinion about what I should do."

"I'll be glad to give you some advice."

"Let me clear the table, bring us some more iced tea, and you can tell me everything you know."

Her willingness to listen made him feel better. Once they'd seated themselves in their comfortable chairs that took up most of the tiny living room, he began. "Usually, new officers are ready to change the lives of every bad guy they run into. They have high ideals and want to write a ticket for every driving infraction they spot." Gordon realized right away he was describing himself when he started out. "Before you head out on a call, make sure the recruit has loaded his gun."

Lizette giggled.

"Don't laugh. It's happened more than once." Thankfully, though he'd done many dumb things as a new recruit, he'd never forgotten to load his weapon.

"While you're driving around, find out what you can about the new guy to help know what you'll be dealing with. If it's a slow day, talking helps pass the time." There was so much more he could tell her, but he felt like she might be bored.

He changed the subject. "Didn't you say you have a couple of movies you wanted to see?"

"Yes, I do. And later we can make banana splits. I have all the ingredients."

Gordon felt less anxious about his wife's assignment and decided to enjoy the rest of their day together.

~ ~ ~

Once they'd returned to the department, Felix and Doug ate the lunch Felix's wife had sent. When they'd finished, Doug called Mr. Portman to see if he'd heard anything from his wife.

Portman's greeting answered Doug's question. "Did you find her? Is she okay?"

"No sir, we haven't learned anything. I hoped she'd have contacted you by now."

"No, and I'm sick with worry. What are you doing to find her?"

"We've sent alerts to the highway patrol and other agencies with descriptions of Mrs. Portman and her car. The information will be on our local news channel, and I'm sure it will be picked up by other television stations right away." Again, the niggling feeling returned. He felt like Portman hadn't told them everything.

"Mr. Portman, I'd like to come over and bring my partner. There are a few more questions I'd like to ask you."

"I've told you everything I can think of, but if you feel it might help...." He let his voice drift off.

"I do, sir. The more I can learn about Mrs. Portman the better."

~ ~ ~

Once they'd entered the foyer, Portman led the way up the flight of stairs. "Would you like to sit at the table again?"

"Yes, that would be fine."

Portman offered coffee, and they took him up on the offer.

Doug gazed out the window at the balcony and the ocean beyond. Having a view like that every day would be great. The ocean could be seen from his home, but nothing like this. The fog had lifted, and sun sparkled on the deep blue of the sea.

Once each of the men had a mug of steaming coffee in front of them, Doug began. "I'd like to know more about your wife. Before you moved here, what were her interests? What did she do to occupy her time?"

Portman blinked. "She belonged to a lot of clubs: a book club, her sorority. She participated in some service events. She enjoyed shopping. I don't know. She always seemed busy."

"What about you?"

"I like to golf. It's kind of an expensive hobby, but I like it. Gives me some exercise."

While Doug asked the questions, Felix took notes of the answers.

"Didn't your wife think she'd miss her clubs?"

"Ventura isn't all that far away. She can keep going to them if she wants. Well, not right now since none of them are meeting because of the virus. I know she hoped to make new friends here, get involved. It hasn't been possible with this COVID going on and all the rules we have to follow. I know she's been disappointed."

Doug felt the need to keep pressing. There had to be more. Some clue to Mrs. Portman's disappearance. "Think hard. There aren't too many places to shop these days. Did she tell you where she intended to go, or what she was looking for?"

Portman's cheeks flushed. "I didn't ask."

"What town do you think she was headed for?"

"My first thought was here in Rocky Bluff, but when she didn't come home in a couple of hours, I guessed Ventura."

Doug felt like asking more questions along the same lines, but Felix changed the subject.

"I'm curious. How long have you two been married?"

Portman's cheeks pinked again. "I'm not good about remembering that stuff. Let me think." He blinked a few more times, clearly embarrassed. "It was several years before I retired. I met Geneva at a friend's house. We were both invited for dinner. Geneva says the host and hostess wanted us to meet. I thought they were merely being nice and wanted to round out the number of guests."

Felix continued with his questions. "How long after that did you two marry?"

"At first, we didn't hit it off. I didn't even ask for her phone number. She called me. Got the number from the friend who had the dinner party. I was surprised but not unhappy about it. I'd been married for a short while, only a couple of years, right after I got out of college. Didn't work out. However, I did miss companionship and a woman's touch in the house." He cleared his throat. "And someone to do my laundry and cook my meals." Portman stared at the French doors.

"I guess it sounds bad, but honestly, when Geneva invited me to go to dinner and a movie with her, I'm being honest when I say those were my first thoughts."

"Does that help you figure out how long you were married?" Felix asked.

"I guess. We only dated for about a year. She was fun and easy to get along with. Plus, she planned everything, and I went along with whatever she thought up for us to do. Easy, and I enjoyed myself and being with her. Getting married seemed like the logical thing to do. We decided the old Ventura Courthouse would be the perfect setting. All our friends came, and we went to Santa Barbara on our honeymoon."

Again, Portman sighed and gazed at the sea. "We've been together for nearly twenty years." He sounded fairly sure.

That brought another question to Doug's mind. "You said you'd been married before. What about Mrs. Portman?"

Portman nodded. "Yes, she'd been married for a long time to a Navy man. He died of a heart attack. Geneva didn't talk about him or their marriage much. I had the feeling it wasn't the happiest situation."

It was getting late, and so far, they hadn't learned anything that might help them find Mrs. Portman. "Sir, could we have a list of your wife's friends and their contact information?"

He pushed himself up by the arms of his chair. "That I can do. She has an address book. It has all of her friends' names in it, their addresses, phone numbers, and their birthdays. You can have it, but you'll need to return it. Geneva uses it all the time."

He moved over to a small desk located in a far corner of the living room. He pulled open the top drawer and brought out a fancy book with a seashell design on the cover. "I think you'll find everything you need here."

Doug hoped the man was right. "One more thing, did you notice your wife acting differently? Moody, maybe?"

"I already told you she was unhappy about not being able to entertain, to see her friends." Portman didn't return to his chair.

Doug knew they were being dismissed.

Chapter 6

When Lizette Butler reported in to the station, she received instructions to meet with Chief Taylor before starting her day as a training officer. The chief still didn't have a permanent secretary, and the first office remained empty except for the solitary desk with a computer on it. Though Lizette had her face mask in her hand, she hadn't put it on. She knocked on the inner door.

"Come in."

She stepped inside. Before she could adjust the mask, the chief said, "Don't bother with that. It drives me crazy not to be able to see people's mouths. We can keep our distance."

Lizette stuffed the mask in her pocket.

Chief Taylor greeted her with a smile and brief nod.

Lizette remained standing, hands at her side, until the chief told her to sit. She noticed the chair was set well away from the desk.

"I wanted to talk a bit about your duties as a training officer and tell you why I chose you to do this job." The chief seldom wore a uniform but had several attractive tailored pant suits which she accented with colorful tops. Today, a bright yellow polka-dotted blouse brightened a smoky-gray jacket and skirt

"Yes, ma'am." She'd already had a lot of instructions from her husband. She hoped she could remember it all.

"First, I wanted you to do it because you're quick to notice flaws men don't tend to notice. I don't want a repeat of our last new hire."

Lizette knew the chief referred to the last new man. He'd crossed the line when it came to contact with pretty women, something Gordon hadn't noticed until Lizette pointed it out.

"We're so understaffed, I want to know if this new recruit has what it takes. Unfortunately, we haven't a lot to choose from. With the political climate like it is, not so many young men and women are interested in a law enforcement career. Plus, we aren't the most desired location for anyone who wants to see a lot of action."

The chief continued. "What I want you to do first is get to know this young man. While you're driving around showing him the city, find out what he's all about."

Exactly what Gordon had told Lizette. "Yes, ma'am."

"Your trainee is waiting for you in the squad room. I know you'll do a great job."

Lizette hoped her boss was right. "Thank you, ma'am."

~ ~ ~

Because they knew they wouldn't be hearing from the medical examiner right away, the detectives decided to concentrate on the Portman case. They'd both gone back to the station after questioning Mr. Portman. They didn't feel they'd learned much, though they had the missing woman's address book.

Doug still had the feeling Portman hadn't shared everything. It was hard to believe the man didn't know more about his wife.

They also needed to find out if they could locate and talk to Lauren Barberick's best friend. It wasn't going to be easy to locate someone with the last name of Johnson.

Doug sat down at his desk. "I'll check the Internet for her name. You can call all the local numbers for Wanda or Harold Johnson."

"What about the address book? Maybe one of us should start on it."

"I've been thinking about that. Don't you think we might find out more if Stacey did it for us? Mrs. Portman's women friends might reluctant to openly discuss their friend with two male police detectives. Women are far more apt to open up to Stacey. Plus, I think she should be the one to call and make appointments to visit Mrs. Portman's friends."

"Good idea."

Using an old telephone directory, Felix flipped it open to the J's. He picked up the phone, got an outside line and dialed.

Doug used his cellphone to contact Stacey. He didn't know if she was still in the building or out in the field.

She answered immediately. "Hi, honey. Is something wrong?"

"No, but I have a job for you. I'll have to clear it with the chief, but I don't think she'll object. I have the missing woman's address book, and I'd like you to make appointments with the women in it and go see them. I think all or most of them are in Ventura."

"What do you want me to find out?"

"Anything one of her friends might know about Mrs. Portman. Has she talked to any of them about problems at home, with her husband, or anyone else? We're looking for anything to help us find her."

"Sure. I'd love to."

When he called and asked, Chief Taylor agreed it was good use of Stacey's time, and it would free the detectives to follow up on the investigation of the family who perished in the house fire.

~~~

All Lizette Butler knew about her trainee was his name: Patrick O'Brien, but she didn't have any trouble spotting him when she entered the squad room. They'd never been a redhaired officer since Stacey had been a part of the department. She knew the broad-shouldered man in the brand-new, crisply creased uniform with the close-cut dark auburn hair had to be her trainee.

Her guess was affirmed when Sergeant Strickland introduced the new recruit. "We're happy to have a new man joining us. Officer O'Brien."

The other men stared at O'Brien, and several spoke welcoming words.

Sergeant Strickland gave a report on the missing woman including her car, he told about the house fire, and mentioned a burglary and other items of interest. He finished his briefing with the usual, "Be careful out there, and keep those face masks on."

As the others rushed toward the door, O'Brien glanced around as though searching for someone.

Lizette approached him. "Hi, I'm Lizette Butler, your training officer. I'd shake hands, but because of the virus we aren't supposed to."

He glanced down at her with his auburn eyebrows raised above his standard-issue face mask. "Oh." He watched the other officers leave the room.

A couple snickered on their way out.

"I'm Officer O'Brien." He extended his hand but withdrew it quickly.

"I guessed. You're the only one in the room I didn't know." She wished she could see more of his face than his light-blue eyes.

"Glad to meet you." His brow furrowed. "Sorry, what was your name again?"

"Butler, but it might be easier to call me Lizette most of the time. My husband is Officer Butler, too. It can get confusing. He's working graveyard now, so it might be a while until you meet him. Let's get going. First, we'll check out a car."

His forehead smoothed.

"You'll need to carry spare face masks. Sometimes they get contaminated." She didn't bother to tell him she'd had someone spit on hers.

"Yes, ma'am."

"Please, call me Lizette."

When they reached their assigned car, Lizette opened the back door. "First thing you want to do is always check out the backseat. Make sure a prisoner didn't leave any surprises." She slipped on a pair of gloves and ran her hand down around the edges of the seat. *Nothing.*

"I've found all sorts of unwanted goodies left behind: a big wad of chewed gum, and once a hypodermic needle. The arresting officer should have discovered it before he put the suspect in the car. Go ahead and look under the seat."

He bent down and peered carefully. "Nothing there." He straightened up.

"Okay, let's get going. Once we're out on the street, we'll let the dispatcher know we're available if needed. Mainly today, I'll be driving you around the city so you can get a feel of where everything is located."

Lizette slid into the driver's seat. He climbed in on the other side, and both fastened their seatbelts.

Lizette started the engine and pulled out of the department lot. She called the dispatcher. "Butler on duty with trainee, O'Brien."

He watched carefully as she used the radio.

"First we'll head down to the beach area." As usual, a bit of fog still drifted in from the ocean. "It'll get sunny soon."

She drove into the big parking lot and told him how once the area held many small houses. "I've been told they once were vacation homes owned by people from the cities. As time went by, they became cheap rentals. Then and now, the beach is a popular spot, especially during summer. But even now, it's used by joggers, and others who enjoy walking along the seashore."

She drove toward the line of new condominiums. "The rentals were demolished and replaced by the condos we're coming up on now."

"Except for the different pastel shades of the outside walls, and what the residents have done in their tiny front yards, they look pretty much the same."

"Yep, but they all have great views of the ocean."

When they drove up to the last building, Lizette pointed. "This is the home of the missing woman Sergeant Strickland mentioned."

They passed the Turf and Tenderloin restaurant, which sat on pilings right at ocean's edge. "This place has been around for a long time. The food is fabulous but pricey. During better times, it's a great place for a special night out. Right now, all you can buy is takeout. Best fish and chips you can get anywhere."

The rookie had been staring out the window at all she'd pointed out, but he hadn't spoken much. *Time to find out something about him.* "Are you married, Patrick?"

"Yes, ma'am."

"Patrick, please, leave the 'ma'ams' for when we're dealing with the public. I'm Lizette. Most everyone goes by their last names, but it's confusing having two Butlers in the department. Do you have any kids?"

"Yes, we have an eight-year old. Sean."

"How do you all like it here so far?"

"Coping with a new place and COVID-19 has made it hard. There's no way for my wife or son to make new friends. My wife keeps busy with the house and helping Sean with his online school work, but having to stay home most of the time has been hard on him."

"What's your wife's name?"

"Molly."

"Maybe we can figure out a way to get-together." Lizette slowed the car as they passed the broken-down pier. "This place is not only an eyesore, but it's dangerous. I have no idea why it hasn't been torn down. Every time we have a big storm, more of it is washed away. Unfortunately, it's a popular place for kids to hang out, and usually not for any good reason."

When they reached the campground, Lizette drove through it. "We seldom have any calls out here. The fellow who owns the place is quite a character and takes care of any problems he might have." Despite it only being mid-April, nearly every camping spot was full. "Looks like some folks have figured out a way to get away from home for a while."

She drove back on Valley Boulevard past the various offices, the bank, stores, and the restaurants, mostly closed. As they drove up the hill, Lizette pointed out all the different streets with names of trees and flowers, giving a bit of information about various crimes that occurred in the past.

Before they drove under the freeway toward the orange orchards and ranches, Lizette asked, "Why did you decide to become a cop?"

"I wanted to be in law enforcement since I was kid. I wanted a job where I could make a difference. Help people, you know."

She could hear his smile even if she couldn't see it. "You went to the police academy in Los Angeles, why didn't you become an officer there?"

"I wanted to, but my wife didn't want me to work in the big city. She thought I'd be in too much danger. Our son was only a few weeks old, so instead, I got a job with the campus police at UCLA."

Lizette asked the obvious question. "So why here now?"

"My desire to be a street cop never left me. I kept checking on advertisement for any department looking for police officers. Most of them were in big cities with as many problems as Los Angeles. I'd nearly given up when I saw the ad from Rocky Bluff. I'd never heard of the place, but the words 'a small beach community' interested me. My wife was willing for me to apply." He shrugged his broad shoulders. "As they say, the rest is history."

With his experience as a campus cop, he might not make the same mistakes someone right out of the academy would. "What kind of crimes did you have to deal with at your former job?"

"The usual: car thefts, burglary, assault, drug violations, domestic violence. The campus was like a city within a city."

When they drove down the road past the ranches and orange groves, O'Brien said, "This section of town is way different than the beach side. It's like a different place."

"Oh, we aren't through yet. There's one other part of Rocky Bluff unlike either of the ones I've showed you so far." She drove down to the place where the fire from the year before had burned out the mobile home park, the abandoned cabins beyond, and the hillside beyond. "A big fire that started in Santa Paula and ended in Santa Barbara came through last year and burned a lot of the hillside."

"I did notice some new building going on right before we went under the overpass. Did the fire burn there, too?"

"Yes. East winds pushed the fire toward town. A change in the direction of the wind made a big difference. If that hadn't happened, the homes all the way to the ocean might have burned down."

Though the radio had been on, no calls were directed toward Lizette. "I'm going to request permission for a meal break. I'll take you to the café cops frequent. Usually I bring my lunch, and it's a good idea while the restaurants have to stay closed. We can still get takeout where we're going. My husband loves their hamburgers."

"I wondered about that. I'll bring my lunch from now on."

"Once you're on your own, you can even go home for lunch if you like."

"That would make Molly and Sean happy."

~ ~ ~

Stacey Butler accepted the challenge of learning more about the missing Geneva Portman with enthusiasm. She studied the missing woman's photograph. As Doug had told her, she was a good-looking woman who'd taken care of herself.

In order to cover as much ground as possible, she decided to call the women in Mrs. Portman's address book and make appointments with them. A couple weren't home, but she was able to make contact with six of the names. None of them admitted to knowing Geneva had been reported missing, and most weren't sure they had any information that would help find her. Despite their answers, Stacey planned to meet with each of them.

Driving to Ventura was always a pleasure. The highway followed the coastline. Stacey was surprised by how many motorhomes and fifth wheels jammed in any place with room to park, despite the fact it was so early in the year.

The first woman on her list, a Pamela Camerena, lived in a white-stucco one-story house on a tree-lined side-street in an old, well-established neighborhood. Though none of the houses were ostentatious, Stacey knew they were worth as much as some of the much bigger homes in Rocky Bluff. A neat lawn, divided by a concrete path, led to a small porch with a decorative overhang. Matching windows with shutters lined either side of a screen door. The inside door stood open.

Stacey rang the bell.

Within seconds, a woman, probably in her late fifties, appeared. Wearing mid-thigh-length white shorts and a green-and-white striped t-shirt, she had a deep tan, emphasized by a cap of short white hair. "Come in, officer. I assume you're the one who called me." Ms. Camerena unlocked the metal screen door.

"Yes, ma'am."

"Come in. The weather is so nice today, I thought you might enjoy sitting on my patio. I made a pitcher of lemonade. Lemons from my tree." She led the way through a small but comfortable living room into a short hallway with closed doors, and down two steps into an area that ran the full width of the house. An arrangement of wicker chairs, tables, and chaise lounges faced a yard filled with fruit trees and flower beds. She pointed toward two chairs with a table between holding a tray with a cut-glass pitcher and two large tumblers.

Ordinarily, Stacey would've declined the offer of refreshment, but in this case, not only would she appreciate the lemonade, it might make the questioning go easier—especially since she could remove her mask to drink, and they would sit on opposite sides of the large, round table. "What a wonderful yard. I don't have time to do much gardening." She sat.

"I love my trees. Not only do they give me great shade, they also provide enough fruit for me to share with the neighbors." Ms. Camerena settled into the chair on the other side of the table after she poured lemonade into both tumblers. "You can take off your mask now. Don't worry. I've been staying home most of the time, always wearing my mask when I have to go shopping."

Stacey didn't hesitate. She stuffed the mask in her pocket and sipped her lemonade. "You know I'm here to try and locate Geneva Portman. How good a friend was she of yours?"

"Best of friends, but I have no idea where she might be. She'd planned to have a housewarming, but of course, this nasty virus has ruined all of our social lives. We still visited often on the phone."

"When was the last time you spoke with her?" Stacey opened her notebook.

"I believe it was Friday morning. We had a normal conversation. Nothing exciting."

"Did she and her husband get along? Any problems you know of?"

Ms. Camerena's laugh came from deep within. "Geneva did mention that with both of them retired and confined to home made her realize how boring her husband is. I'm laughing because I agree. He's a retired college professor, taught history, and that seems to be all he can talk about. Geneva said now his favorite subjects are all the previous pandemics the world has experienced, including the statistics of how many died."

"Did she say whether or not she had any ideas as to how she might change things? Something that might hint where she went?"

"Not really. If Anthony, her husband, was missing I'd be inclined to think she might have done away with him." Again, the low laugh.

"How much do you know about your friend's private life? Did she have any affairs? Anything out of the ordinary?"

"We're all a bit old for that sort of shenanigans. When she lived here, Geneva played tennis and belonged to all the same clubs we all did. Our big excitement was going to an elegant restaurant for a great meal." She paused. "Wonder if any of our favorite restaurants will survive."

"How long have you known Geneva?"

"Hmm." Ms. Camerena thought for a moment. "For at least fifteen years. Before my husband had a heart attack and passed away."

Stacey asked a few more questions and finished her lemonade. "It's time for me to see a few more of Geneva's friends."

"Who's next?"

"Carrie Dunlap."

"You won't learn anything more than I've told you from her. The one you need to see is Kiersten Bishop. She's even better friends with Geneva than I am. They go back all the way to grade school. If Geneva had any dark secrets, Kiersten is the one who'd know about them."

Chapter 7

After receiving some unsettling news, Chief Chandra Taylor called Devon Duvall, Rocky Bluff's mayor. Chandra and Devon's relationship continued to be a difficult one, partly because of Devon's recently acquired daughter, Kayla, and partly because of dealing with the new rulings about the virus.

Devon answered immediately. "I'm almost afraid to ask you why you called. Is it foolish to hope you have good news?"

"I'm afraid so. I'm sure you're aware of the not-so-peaceful protests happening around the country."

"I guess I'm not going to like what I'm about to hear."

"You probably won't. I've been getting bulletins from other nearby police departments concerning how outside agitators are actually paying people to protest."

"I've heard that, too."

"The latest is they now plan to focus on small towns."

"Specifically, Rocky Bluff?"

"No, not yet. However, I want to have a plan in place in case we hear that Rocky Bluff may be targeted. We are so understaffed that protecting our city won't be easy."

"I hope you're not asking for more money for hiring because we don't have it right now."

"No, no. What I want is for us to get together and see if we can think of some ideas. If we come up with anything, you might need to run it by the city council."

Devon didn't speak for a full minute. Then he sighed. "As you know, we're down in numbers on the council, and frankly, I don't know how much good they'd be in making any meaningful decisions. We can't even have a regular council meeting with members of the community attending. There's not enough room to do the required social distancing."

"What I really want is for you and me to get together and exchange ideas. Once we have some potential plans, I can run it by key people in the department. We may not have a problem, but it's far better to be prepared." To be perfectly honest, Chandra wanted to see Devon. It had been too long since they'd spent any time together.

"I'm ready. I miss you. Where and when?"

"Could you come to my office? Sometime today, preferably."

"How about noon? I'll pick up some takeout."

"Great. I'll leave word at the front desk." For the first time in days, Chandra felt excited in a good way. Though at times she thought any kind of meaningful relationship with Devon had been doomed from the time she learned he had a teenaged daughter he hadn't told her about. She'd come to accept the reason he'd not mentioned Kayla was because the girl's mother had not allowed him to spend any time with their daughter, nor even kept in touch with him until she realized cancer would take her life.

Chandra had come to care for Kayla. It hadn't been easy for the girl to live with a father she didn't know. The transition had been difficult, and Chandra felt she'd been a help during the worst of it.

~~~

Doug and Felix had called every Johnson in the phone directory, and nearly everyone they found on the Internet who lived in the general area in their effort to locate Wanda Johnson, the friend of the deceased Lauren Barberick. When Doug called the number of a Larry Johnson, he received no answer.

"I guess we'll have to wait until tonight to see if we can catch him at home." He'd no sooner hung up, when his office phone rang again. "Detective Milligan."

"I was told to speak with you. I just heard about a fire at my friend's house. Is it true? Lauren and her kids died in the fire?"

"Who is this speaking?" Doug asked.

"Oh, sorry. I'm afraid I'm not thinking straight since I heard about the fire. This is Wanda Johnson. Lauren is my best friend."

Doug pointed to the phone and mouthed, "Wanda Johnson."

Felix picked up the extension on his desk.

"Yes, Mrs. Johnson. Thanks for calling."

"I prefer Ms. I've been happily free of my husband for over six years. Please tell me about the fire."

"Would you be more comfortable if we came to your home?"

"No. I'm not there. I'm what they consider an essential worker. I'm a clerk at the grocery store. Please tell me about Lauren and the kids."

"It's not good news, I'm afraid. The whole family perished in the fire."

She gasped. "That bastard husband of hers did it. You need to arrest him."

"Ma'am, he expired in the fire, too."

"Good." She sounded like she'd started to cry.

"Ma'am, could you please tell me why you think he was the one who started the fire?"

It took a moment for her to answer. "I can't believe Lauren is gone and those darling children, too."

"Do you want us to come to where you are? It might be easier to speak with us there." He could tell the woman was having a hard time."

She sniffed a few times. "I don't think I can leave right now. We're really busy. My lunch break is at one. Could you come to the market? We could talk in the break room. You'll have to wear a mask, and we'll have to sit six feet apart. Our manager is really fussy about all the rules."

"No problem. My partner and I will see you at one."

Felix glanced at his watch. "We might as well eat before we go." He opened the bottom drawer of his desk and lifted out a thermal bag. "You bring something? "

"Yep. Stacey packed us both a lunch. I'll get mine."

"Have you heard from your wife? Wonder how she's doing with her interviews."

"Nothing yet. Hope it's a good sign."

~~~

Felix Zachary's wife, Wendy, spent the morning preparing online work with her students in her class and doing her Zoom classes. Fortunately, since she found herself even busier putting together work for her kids at school and working with them online, her mother and mother-in-law continued to take turns caring for their granddaughter, Ruby. When most people who worked from home dressed in sweats or stayed in pajamas, because Wendy's students could see her when she taught them, she always made sure her blonde hair was nicely arranged, and she wore nice outfits every day, even though she often padded around on bare feet.

"You seem worried, Wendy. Is something wrong?" Her mother's eyes showed her concern.

Wendy knew her mother remembered back to when post-partum depression had enveloped her daughter. "Nothing you can fix, Mom. It's this situation with school.

It's a lot more difficult to teach when you can't be with the kids. This semester will be over soon, but I wonder what will happen in the fall."

"Surely by then, this virus will be gone and everything will be back to normal."

"I don't know, Mom. The number of cases keeps climbing, even right here in Rocky Bluff. And if school does open, kids and teachers will get sick. Even before the virus, it's what always happens at the beginning of school."

Ruby, the toddler, a true combination of her mother and father with her cocoa-colored skin, light eyes, and curly, light-brown hair, came running in. "Gammy, come play with me." Her grandmother scooped the child up in her arms and made kissing noises behind her mask as she put her face against the child's plump rosy cheek. "Of course, I will." She glanced at Wendy. "I wish we could do play dates again. Ruby needs to have friends."

"Much too dangerous right now."

Wendy's mother sighed and carried Ruby off in the direction of the playroom.

When Felix and Wendy decided to marry, both sets of parents were against it. They heard plenty of arguments "Mixing races is never a good idea, if you have children it will be hard on them." "They won't know if they are white or African American."

Even after the marriage, Felix's parents snubbed Wendy, and her parents weren't any better to Felix. When Ruby arrived, everything changed, slowly at first, but certainly the family dynamics became much better.

Wendy knew her mother couldn't really grasp what was going on. She didn't accept how bad the virus was. The only reason she and her husband wore a mask in public was because if she didn't, Wendy would have kept them from seeing Ruby. Felix's folks seemed to understand the situation better and never argued about wearing their masks when visiting or caring for Ruby.

Both sets however, had expressed the opinion the greatest threat to exposure to the virus came from Felix since he was around the public all the time. Wendy worried about it, too, but Felix kept his clothes in the garage, washed what could be washed, took his other clothing to the cleaners himself, and showered before he spent any time with Wendy or Ruby.

There was too much for Wendy to think about right now. *Best to get busy with planning tomorrow's lessons.*

~~~

Devon Duval entered Chandra's office holding up bags containing what smelled like green chilis and tortillas.

"Brought tostados from Gabriela's Mexican Restaurant." He set the bags down on Chandra's desk. Gabriela Ontiveros was one of the council members and owned two restaurants and a gift shop.

"Great. Haven't had Mexican food for a long time." Chandra cleared her desk and began to set out their food. "How are things going at city hall?"

"We're not really open. Everyone has to take care of business via the Internet or by phone. And believe me, both are busy." He accepted a container with a huge tostada. "There's some roasted chilis and chips and salsa in there somewhere, too."

Delicious food. Chandra savored every bite. *Wonderful to be enjoying a meal with Devon.* She glanced at him. *So handsome, unblemished dark skin, big intelligent brown eyes with the longest lashes, a nose the right size for his face, and the perfectly shaped mouth.* "What is the biggest problem you're dealing with?"

"The businesses that can't be open right now. All the owners are complaining. It's the reason I picked up food from Gabriela's restaurant. I've been going back and forth between both: Mexican one night, Chinese the next. I can't do anything about her gift shop." Gabriela also owned Seaside Gifts and Guns, definitely a non-essential business by the governor's standards.

She and Devon finished and cleaned up her desk. "That was wonderful, thank you. Time to get to the business I called you here to discuss."

Chapter 8

Chandra folded her hands on her desk. "We're intercepting messages about so-called peaceful demonstrations being planned for the smaller beach cities. I don't know if it's true, but supposedly there is financing to bring in outsiders. Outsiders who have no intention of being peaceful."

"What is it you think might happen?" A slight line marred Devon's handsome face as he stared at her.

"The wrong kind of people could play havoc here. I worry about our businesses being broken into and looted. They are all having troubles enough. And if many come, no doubt they'll do some damage to homes too." She paused. "We don't have the manpower to protect all of Rocky Bluff. Our biggest problem is we have three areas to oversee: this part of the city, the homes on the bluff, and the ranches on the other side of the highway."

"What about asking our citizens to help?"

Chandra grimaced. "Only as a last resort. If untrained people help, it could easily turn violent. I'm hoping if we both think hard, we can come up with a workable plan."

Devon spread out his hands. "Wow. I'm not sure there is one. When is this all supposed to happen?"

"So far, there have been no definitive rumors of day or time. Not really a place pinpointed either. I have my best computer guy keeping track of all the messages coming in. What I'm hoping is we can come up with something before anything happens."

"Have you asked any of your people for solutions?"

"Not yet. It's my next step."

"I'll think about it, but I doubt I can come up with anything useful. Wow. Scary. Do you want me to say anything to the council members?" Devon asked.

"It's up to you."

"I doubt they'll have any ideas about what to do, but they should be notified about what we may be up against."

~~~

Stacey saw two more of Geneva Portman's friends before her appointment with Kiersten Bishop. She'd sounded suspicious when Stacey first contacted her, and asked a myriad of questions about the circumstances. When Stacey told Ms. Bishop her friend was missing, she'd agreed to talk.

Kiersten Bishop's small home perched on the side of a hill near the old courthouse. The best thing about the house was the view of the city and the ocean from the huge window in the living room. The inside, decorated for comfort rather than flair, held several overstuffed chairs overflowing with pillows and facing the vista. Small tables sat between the seating. All shades of blue made-up the color scheme.

Wearing her mask and keeping an appropriate distance, after simple introductions, Stacey sat in the place Ms. Bishop indicated.

"How can I help you?" Ms. Bishop settled her plump self into one of the chairs turned a bit toward Stacey's. Her long white hair was clipped at the nape of her neck with a silver barrette. Though she was probably in her late fifties or early sixties, few wrinkles marred her smooth skin. She wore a printed caftan in shades of blue that covered all but her dimpled elbows and sandaled feet.

Though Stacey would have liked to remove it, she kept her mask on. "I'd like to hear anything you know about Geneva Portman that might help us locate her." Stacey opened her notebook, her pen poised.

"Geneva is and has been my best friend since high school. I probably know more about her than anyone, but I'm not going to share any gossip about her."

"I'm not here for gossip. However, if there is something you know that might help us locate Mrs. Portman, please tell me. Her husband doesn't seem to have any idea what might have happened to her."

"Of course not. He hardly pays any attention to what she has to say. They seem to get along okay, but in my opinion, theirs is a marriage of convenience on both sides. I wouldn't call it the great love affair. Have you met Anthony?"

"No, ma'am. What can you tell me about him?"

"A college professor when Geneva met him, and fairly handsome at the time. Made good money, and according to Geneva, he has been wise with his investment plus a good retirement. I think the fact that he could support her and is always generous was a big part of the attraction on her side. She'd had a bit of a rough spell after her first husband died." She stared out at the horizon. "To be honest, Anthony has about as much personality as a toad."

She shook her head. "Maybe that's not fair, but I know he doesn't care much for the same things Geneva does. Geneva enjoys a good time. He went along with her, but it was obvious he was often bored and clearly would have been happier staying home."

Whether Kiersten Bishop stuck to facts or added her own feelings didn't matter. A picture of Geneva Portman's life began to form. "Do you think your friend meant to leave her husband?"

Ms. Bishop shook her head. "Last time we spoke she was thrilled with her new home, and when this stupid plague is over, she planned to have a big housewarming. None of us has had a chance to visit her yet." She ran her hands over her long white hair. "And as far as I know she had no plan to leave her husband. She, and all the rest of us, are at a stage in life we're ready to accept where we are and what we've become. Geneva has been with her husband a long time. If she planned to make a change, she never expressed it to me."

"Since she moved, has she visited you or do you know of anyone else she may have visited?"

"Until the virus, our group managed to get-together at least a couple of times a month. Sometimes during the day, at others, meeting at a nice restaurant for dinner."

Stacey felt like she'd learned all she could from Ms. Bishop. "Thank you." She closed her notebook and started to rose.

"Wait, there's one more thing I should mention."

Stacey settled back down.

Ms. Bishop didn't speak for a long moment. "What I'm going to say borders on gossip, but I'd feel terrible if it turned out to be important." She stood and walked toward the window, the long skirt of her caftan swishing around her ankles.

She turned and pursed her lips. "When Geneva was still married to her first husband, she had an affair. It didn't last long, but I remember the man wasn't at all happy about her decision to end it. He threatened to tell her husband. Geneva beat him to it, and told him herself."

"Did she have anything more to say about this other man? "

"The reason I'm telling you is because she told me she'd recently seen her old lover."

Intriguing. "Was she interested in getting back with him?"

"Absolutely not, in fact the opposite. She hoped he hadn't spotted her. She seemed upset."

"Did she say where this happened?"

"Yes, in Rocky Bluff, that's why it bothered her so much."

"What can you tell me about this man?"

"His name is Roger Endicott. Way back when the affair started, I saw him with Geneva several times. Back then, he was movie-star handsome, dark-haired, tanned, great physique, and self-assured. What he looks like now, I have no idea. I didn't ask."

Stacey wrote the name down in her notebook. "Why would it upset her to run into him now after such a long time?"

"Now we're getting into territory I really don't like to discuss. Because it was such a long time ago, I'm not sure my memory about what I saw and heard is all that good."

"Anything you can tell me might help us locate your friend. We really have nothing else to go on." Stacey hoped her words might encourage Ms. Bishop.

"The last time I saw Geneva and Roger together, I ran into them at a restaurant at the beach. Neither of them seemed happy. I wasn't sure if it was because I'd seen them, or if something else was going on." She frowned. "It wasn't too long afterward when Geneva told me she'd broken up with him."

"You said he wasn't happy about her decision?"

"No, according to Geneva, he didn't take it well at all."

Chapter 9

Though the manager of the grocery store wasn't pleased, he led Doug and Felix to the back of the building and pointed out the break room. "This better not take long. I need Wanda's help. Got too many employees out sick or too scared of the virus to come to work."

Doug opened the door, and both detectives entered.

A young woman with dark hair piled atop her head in a messy knot, wearing a dark blue apron with the store's red logo, over a red short-sleeved shirt, and blue jeans sat at a square table. In front of her, an opened paper napkin held a half-eaten sandwich, and an empty bag of chips, with a soda can nearby. "Oh, you must be the detectives."

"Yes, ma'am." Both Doug and Felix showed her their IDs.

"Please sit. I guess you figured out I'm Hannah's friend, Wanda Johnson." She pointed to the chairs across from her. "I'd offer you some coffee, but my boss made it, and it's awful."

"We're fine." Felix pulled out a chair on the opposite side of the table from Ms. Johnson, as did Doug.

She took a sip of her soda, wiped her mouth with a napkin, wadded it up, and tossed it and the can into a nearby trash can. "I hope I can talk about Hannah and the kids without bursting into tears. Whenever I think about them, I cry."

"How much did you know about her marriage?" Doug opened his notebook.

Ms. Johnson shrugged and sighed. "It was terrible. Jim was a monster. Poor Hannah. She didn't feel like she could leave him because of the kids. I tried to convince her she should. He didn't care about those kids anyway, at least not the two oldest, Caleb and Caroline. They belonged to Hannah's first husband, who died in a car accident. Of course, when Jim romanced her, he acted like he thought the world of those kids. And that's what it was, nothing but an act."

Ms. Johnson gazed off, her eyes moist with tears. "Give me a moment. I loved those beautiful kids. Took care of them a lot."

Doug waited until the woman wiped her eyes. "The baby belonged to Mr. Barberick?"

"Yes, and she was the only one of the kids he treated decently, a darling girl, only nine months old. She was the main reason Hannah hadn't left Jim. She knew he'd fight like crazy for custody."

"Did Mr. Barberick ever threaten his wife?"

"Hannah didn't like to talk about it, but yes, and I was present when he did it. He even threatened me. Told me he didn't want me around Hannah and the kids and if I kept coming, I'd be sorry. He couldn't keep us from meeting elsewhere or stop us from chatting on the phone or exchanging emails." The tears flowed once again.

Ms. Johnson sniffed and dabbed at her eyes. "He took her phone away, but her folks got her another. She kept it hidden from him."

Doug felt Ms. Johnson had told them enough for them to make Jim Barberick the main suspect for setting the fire. Why he died in it, too, would have to come from the arson investigators. "Thank you so much, Ms. Johnson. You've been most helpful."

She sighed. "I'm still having trouble processing what happened. Hannah was my best friend."

~ ~ ~

Stacey returned to the station not long after her husband and Felix got back. She went to their office to let them know what she'd learned about Geneva Portman.

When she opened the door, Doug grinned and got out of his seat. "Hope you have some information for us." He unfolded one of two chairs they kept for guests. Their two desks nearly filled their tiny space.

She sat. "Not as much as I hoped for, though I did learn a lot about Mrs. Portman. None her friends I interviewed had any idea where she might be."

"That's disappointing." Felix crossed his long legs.

"What about her marriage? Any problems there?" Doug asked.

"From what her friends told me, her marriage to Mr. Portman was fine if not the most exciting. She'd been married before and she had an affair. Despite the fact the romance ended years ago, Mrs. Portman spotted this man in Rocky Bluff and, from what her friends said, wasn't happy about it."

Doug leaned forward. "Could be a good lead. Did you find out his name?"

"Roger Endicott."

"Anyone mention anything else about her marriage with Portman?"

"Not really. Though none of her friends thought he was the most exciting man, no one mentioned any troubles between the two."

"Anyone say if Mr. Portman knew about this Endicott guy?"

"No. From what I could gather, the affair happened long before she met and married her latest husband."

Doug turned toward Felix. "Let's see what we can find out about this Endicott, and we should visit Portman again."

"On it." Felix started working on his computer.

Stacey stood. "I'll write up what I learned and get it to you."

"Thanks, sweetheart, see you at home."

~~~

Didn't take long for Felix to find out Endicott had a clean record, except for some traffic citations. His last known address was in Santa Barbara. Felix jotted it down. "When do you want to check him out?"

"Let's visit Portman first and see if he's ever heard about Endicott and the affair." Doug stood and grabbed his jacket off the back of the chair.

~~~

The fog had completely burned off and the temperature rose to a pleasant mid-seventies. The strong, salty scent from the ocean drifted in on a breeze.

When Doug called Portman, he asked if they'd found his wife. He sounded disappointed by Doug's negative answer. When Doug asked if they could stop by to ask a few more questions, his response was, "Of course, but I can't think of anything I haven't already told you."

Portman greeted the two detectives at the door. His demeanor was hard to decipher. Doug couldn't tell by his expression whether he was irritated by their visit or merely more worried about his wife.

"Come on up. I'm not sure how I can help you anymore than I have." Portman huffed and puffed his way up the stairs.

Doug didn't explain the reason for the repeat visit until the three of them had settled in their now-accustomed places at the dining room table. "I'd like to know more about your wife's past."

Portman's face gathered into a puzzlement of wrinkles. "What exactly do you mean? Her childhood I know very little about, or even her growing up years."

"What about her first marriage?"

Portman's eyes opened wide. He appeared startled. "What does that have to do with anything?"

"Could be a lot. "Felix had his notebook and pen out.

Portman hunched his shoulders. "The marriage was over long before Geneva and I got together. At least before we started seeing one another on a regular basis."

"What did she tell you about the marriage?"

"I only know it didn't end on a happy note."

"Do you know why?"

Portman blinked a few times. "No, and I didn't care."

Felix jotted a few notes. "Did you have anything to do with the break-up?"

"Heavens no. Like I said, it ended long before Geneva and I were even seeing one another." Portman crossed his arms over his chest. "I never met her first husband. Can't even remember his name. Geneva did tell me he left the area as soon as they were divorced. That's it. I don't know anything else."

Doug wasn't ready to give up. "Didn't she ever mention what happened? Seems like you might have been curious."

Portman's cheeks took on a crimson shine. "I don't know how many times I have to say I don't know. I didn't care. I was thrilled she agreed to marry me. There's isn't anything more I can add."

Doug didn't believe him, but knew Portman wasn't going to add anymore. "Did you ever hear of someone named Roger Endicott?"

Portman shook his head. "No. Who is that?"

"You're sure your wife never mentioned him?" Doug studied Portman for any reaction.

"Should I know this person?" Portman lifted his eyebrows. "Honestly, I've never heard the name before. Did he have something to do with my wife's disappearance?"

"We don't know. The name was mentioned by one of your wife's friends."

"Who is he, anyway?"

"Probably not anyone important."

This seemed to satisfy Portman.

When Doug and Felix started to get up, Portman said, "There is one thing I haven't mentioned."

Doug exchanged a glance with his partner. "What's that?"

"I didn't want to say anything, because it seems silly now."

Felix leaned forward. "What? It's important that you tell us everything."

Portman cleared his throat. "I don't think it's important, but Geneva seemed a bit agitated the last couple of days."

"What do you mean by agitated?" *Oh, for Pete's sake, why hadn't the man mentioned this before?*

"It's hard to explain. Geneva usually chattered a lot about what she planned or wanted to do. And like I said, I wasn't very good about paying attention to her, not because I didn't care," he shrugged, "but because she was going to do what she wanted no matter what I said. It didn't matter, I only wanted her to be happy."

"So, what was different than normal?" Felix had a twinge of annoyance in his voice.

Portman rubbed his hands together. "Maybe agitated isn't the best description. She wasn't acting like herself. But lately she hasn't been as talkative as usual. Her mind seemed to be elsewhere. And I hate to admit it, but I kind of enjoyed the quiet."

Doug suspected Portman might be feeling guilty for not telling them this before. "Thank you, sir. I'm not sure that's important, but it might be."

Next, they'd see if they could find Roger Endicott at home.

Chapter 10

After Lizette and her trainee had finished eating lunch, she drove him up to the neighborhood on the bluffs. All of the homes were much larger and on bigger lots than those in the neighborhood by the beach.

"Wow. I had no idea these classy homes were up here." Patrick O'Brien made comments about houses as they passed by. "Many burglaries up here?"

"A few. Many of the homeowners have alarm systems of some kind. When there is a burglary, it's often because someone forgot to turn on their alarm. During Christmas, when lots of packages were stolen off front porches, people bought outside cameras. Not sure it stopped potential thieves, but did help us identify a few and make some arrests."

"I've wondered if the coronavirus has slowed down crime or if wearing masks has given criminals more guts."

"Crime is down a bit. I guess the virus scares everyone." She drove past the large Rocky Bluff Community Church. "This is the church my family and I attend."

"Wow. That must be the biggest church in town." Patrick stared out the window. "Certainly bigger than the Catholic Church we passed earlier."

"We're having outdoor services. No contact, we sit in our own cars."

"I'll let my wife know. She misses our old church."

Lizette continued to drive toward the homes near the edge of the bluff. "Tell me, Patrick, what do you and your wife like to do in your spare time?"

Patrick snickered. "Something you'd never guess. We love to bake cookies and come up with new recipes. We've created a new chocolate chip cookie. It's fabulous. I'll bring you a dozen and you can share with your husband."

What a surprise, a cop who liked to bake cookies. "That would be great. I love cookies and don't seem to have much time to bake."

"We have a secret ingredient. You'll be surprised how good these taste."

"I can hardly wait. Once all this craziness is over, we'll have your family come to dinner. I'll cook some Filipino dishes, my specialty."

"So, does this mean you're Filipino?"

"Yes, plus a mix of Native American and Anglo. With your name and looks, I suspect you're mainly Irish."

"Mostly, though my wife did both of our DNA. We have a bit from other European countries as well. My Scottish ancestry is a tad more than the Irish."

Lizette stared at him for a moment. With his deep auburn hair, blue eyes, and fair skin, he looked more Irish than anything else.

Patrick chuckled. "My wife has more DNA from Ireland than I do, and she's got black hair, and a bit darker skin color."

"I'm anxious to meet your wife. Molly's her name, right?"

He nodded. "She wants to meet you, too."

"We'll figure out a way for it to happen."

They'd neared the oldest homes perched on the edge of the bluff. "There's something I want to show you." She parked the car. "We'll get out here."

Patrick's expression revealed his curiosity.

"This may come in handy for you one day, but you're also going to see something beautiful. Put on your mask in case we run into someone."

She led him down a narrow path between two fenced-off homes. When they reached the end, a waist-high brick wall had been built along the edge of the bluff. The ocean was filled with whitecaps atop the waves as they rolled in. The Channel Islands could be seen easily.

"Wow, what a view."

"Glad it's so clear. Sometimes it's too foggy to see the islands." She turned. "Let's go this way." She led him down the path behind several more houses. Most of them were surrounded by fences, usually low enough to see into elegant yards. A few of the homes backed right up to the path, with large windows and balconies facing the sea. Concrete benches were placed strategically along the path.

After they'd passed several of these homes, there was another space with a path leading to the street. "We'll come out through this one. There are four more openings like this. All of these houses were built a long time ago, mostly white stucco with red tile roofs, much like the homes in Santa Barbara." She went on to explain the houses lining the bluff had been built before anyone else had moved there. "My guess is the lot owners planned this to be their own small community."

"Do you have much crime up here?" Patrick followed Lizette out to the street.

"More than you'd expect. Like I said, burglaries mainly, but remember the big white church we passed?

The minister's wife was murdered, though it didn't happen here."

Patrick's eyes grew larger.

"I'll tell you about it sometime and some other stories about people who live up here."

The radio interrupted their conversation. The dispatcher reported a crime for them to investigate.

"Okay, we've got a job to do right here on the bluff. A garage has been burglarized."

Patrick grinned. "Cool." His expression changed. "Well not so good for the homeowner, but I'm glad we get to be useful."

The address was only four blocks away, and it was easy enough to know where to go because a middle-aged woman wearing a business suit jumped up and down and waved her arms in huge arcs. A mask with flowers printed on it covered the bottom half of her face. A new Jeep was parked in front of an open garage. The house, a sprawling one-story, set back from the street, with a deep green lawn in front.

Not taking the time to make a U-turn, Lizette parked the wrong way close to the driveway. Both she and Patrick got out and approached the woman.

She ran straight to Patrick. "Oh, officer, I'm so glad you got here so quickly. I can't believe it. Someone broke into my garage and stole a bunch of stuff, mainly my husband's tools and his golf clubs. I came home early from work because I wanted to do some grocery shopping and drove up and used my remote, but when I started to drive in, I could tell something was wrong." She gestured toward the open garage. "My husband is going to have a fit. I don't know how this could've happened."

Patrick glanced toward Lizette. She nodded a go-ahead, and took out her notebook and pen.

"Did you touch anything, ma'am?"

"I only took one step inside, far enough to see. That's how I realized George's, that's my husband, stuff was missing."

"Good. We'll check for fingerprints. Did you see anyone around here when you drove up?"

She shook her head. "Not a soul. Everyone on this block works during the daytime. At least I think they do. I've never seen anyone around when I've been home."

"Do you have an alarm system or surveillance cameras?"

"No, we moved in less than two months ago, and though we've talked about it, we haven't had a security system installed."

Lizette stepped toward the open garage. She'd never seen such a neat interior in a garage. The cement floor was immaculate. Both side walls contained shelving with only a few tools. Boxes with writing on them were stacked against the back.

The homeowner had her cellphone in her hand. "I'd better call my husband."

"Before you do, please give me your name and phone number," Patrick said.

"Emily Garrett, but everyone calls me Emmy." She rattled off her phone number.

After jotting down the information, Lizette asked, "How well do you know your neighbors, Mrs. Garrett?"

"Hardly at all. We've been too busy getting settled to socialize much, though my husband has gone to the golf course in Ventura. We moved from there and still see our friends." She ran her fingers through her frizzy graying bob. "Are you suggesting maybe a neighbor did this? Surely not, everyone up here has to be fairly well-off to afford to live here."

"We're not going to rule anyone out as yet." Lizette moved closer to the garage.

"What about your remote?" Patrick pointed to the one in Mrs. Garrett's hand "When you got in the car to come home was it where you always put it?"

Mrs. Garrett blinked her mascaraed lashes. "I don't remember. I think so. Why do you ask?"

Lizette wondered, too.

"I investigated a similar case where I once worked. Go ahead and call your husband. You probably should call your insurance company, too. Once we check the garage, you'll want to make a list of all the missing items for them and us." Patrick started back for their car. "I'll get our fingerprint kit."

So far, this new recruit was turning out to be an asset.

~~~

Hopefully Roger Endicott would be home, and they could ask him about his relationship with Geneva Portman. Then Doug and Felix could go home for dinner. Doug didn't expect to learn anything meaningful from Endicott but hoped he might be mistaken.

They drove up the 101 toward Santa Barbara. The Channel Islands could be seen clearly. Doug spotted a few people surfing in the rolling waves heading toward shore. "What a great afternoon it turned out to be. Guess those guys out there riding the waves aren't concerned about catching the virus."

Their car's GPS took them into the downtown area of Santa Barbara and into an older neighborhood close to the main shopping area. The address they sought turned out to be a small yellow house with a white picket fence. A FOR SALE sign decorated the pocket-sized front lawn.

"This might not be as simple as I'd hoped." Doug stepped out of the car.

"Cute house. Probably won't last long."

"Let's hope our guy is home."

Knocking and ringing the bell raised no one inside the house.

On their way back to the street, someone hollered. "Yoo hoo. If you're looking for Roger, he hasn't been around for a while."

The person beckoning was an old, tiny, white-haired woman, leaning against the fence on the far side of the Endicott home. "I'm Mrs. Honeywell, and Roger's been my neighbor for the last five years."

"Perhaps you could answer a few questions for us." Doug let himself out the gate and approached the elderly woman. "I'm Detective Milligan, and my partner is Detective Zachary."

"Is Roger in some kind of trouble?" Mrs. Honeywell moved toward them. Curiosity seemed to glitter from her faded blue eyes.

Doug wondered why she hadn't asked if something had happened to her neighbor. "No, we'd merely like to ask him a few questions."

"About some woman or other, I'll bet." She tucked her brown speckled hands into the pockets of the baggy jeans she wore.

"Why would you say that?" Felix asked.

"He loved the ladies. Brought a lot of different ones home."

You could always count on older persons in the neighborhood to keep tabs on the comings and goings of the people around them. "If I showed you a photo of one, do you think you might remember if she is one of the women you saw?"

"My eyesight isn't all that good anymore, but I'll be happy to take a look."

Doug got out his phone and found the picture of Geneva Portman. He moved close enough to show it to Mrs. Honeywell. He caught a whiff of lavender and what smelled like baby powder.

She squinted. "She looks like a nice lady. Not the type Roger cavorted with."

"Does that mean you've never seen this woman?"

"I wouldn't swear to it. She could've been here. There's been a passel of them coming and going."

"Where do you think we might find Mr. Endicott?" Doug put his phone back in his pocket.

"Not here. He put his house up for sale, and he moved all his stuff out."

"Do you know where he went?"

"No. We weren't on speaking terms."

"Is there anything else you might tell us?" Felix moved toward the FOR SALE sign. "Has he had any luck with the sale of his house?"

"Oh, yes, indeed. A nice little family bought it. The real-estate lady stopped by yesterday and told me I'd soon have new neighbors and I'd love them. Honestly, it'll be nice not to imagine Roger's lifestyle anymore."

Doug gave Mrs. Honeywell his card. "If you happen to think of anything else, you might tell us about Mr. Endicott give me a call."

Doug waited until they were inside the car to say he wasn't sure if they should believe everything Mrs. Honeywell said about her neighbor.

"I think you might be right. She struck me as kind of a busybody. I checked the FOR SALE sign and took down the realtor's phone number. Want to give her a call?"

"Let's wait until tomorrow. I'm ready to call it a day."

Chapter 11

Lizette and Patrick took a lot of time taking fingerprints off the garage door opener, the driver's door of the Jeep, and any other place they thought someone could have touched. However, most likely, whoever had robbed the Garretts' garage had worn gloves.

While they worked, Patrick explained he'd worked on a similar case at his former job at the college. "Some of the professors lived in housing near the campus, and we had a rash of garage burglaries. It turned out one of the students figured out the routines of each of the professors on the weekends. In one case, the victim regularly went to a local gym. The student followed him, got into his car, lifted the garage door remote, closed the door without locking it, and used the remote to get into the garage. He'd steal what he wanted, leave, and return the remote to the car. Finally, a neighbor caught him in the act and called the police. My guess is something similar probably happened here."

"You think someone who lives in the neighborhood is the guilty party?"

"Probably."

A most unhappy Mr. Garrett came home while they worked. "I hope you catch the dirty S.O.B. who did this." He jammed his fists into the pockets of his slacks.

Lizette told him he and Mrs. Garrett should go to the police station to leave have their fingerprints taken for comparison to what they'd gotten from the crime scene.

"We'll be happy to do whatever it takes." He shook his head. "I want my stuff back."

The insurance agent showed up when they were ready to leave. Both the agent and the Garretts promised to give Lizette a list of what was missing.

Lizette didn't think there was much of a chance that the items would be recovered.

"Time to go in. We'll make our reports and head home."

~~~

Lizette brought take-home Chinese food for Gordon's and her dinner. Since it was so late, there wouldn't be enough time for her to cook the kind of meal she usually did. Plus, she really wanted to share with Gordon about the time she'd spent with her trainee.

Gordon was dressed and ready for his shift. "You're way later than usual. Did you have problems today?" He used chopsticks to eat the moo goo gai pan he'd put on top of the rice he'd piled on his plate.

Lizette had used chopsticks her entire life, but the amount of food Gordon could get into his mouth with one grasp of the sticks amazed her. "No problem with my trainee, he's a great guy. Family man and likes to bake cookies."

Gordon's chopsticks paused in midair. "Cookies? What kind of guy does that?"

"Patrick and his wife like to make-up recipes for different kinds of cookies. He's promised to make some for us." She'd known Gordon would be as surprised as she was by Patrick's hobby. "They have a son."

"Family man. That's good. I take it he's nothing like the last new guy."

"Nope. Worked as a campus cop before he came here. Even had a similar experience to a call we had to take. Garage burglary on the bluff."

"Didn't you turn it over to the detectives?" Gordon polished off most of what was on his plate and dished up some chow mein.

"We filed our report, and I called Doug. He told me to go ahead and investigate it ourselves. We can give him a call if we need help."

"That's a surprise. What are you going to do next?"

"Patrick thinks it could be a neighbor who did it. Maybe someone lost his job and is home and watched our victim leaving the house." Lizette filled in the details about the burglary. She paused to eat some of the broccoli beef.

Though she knew Gordon wanted to hear what their plans were for their investigation, the food kept him occupied.

She finally continued. "The victims are new to Rocky Bluff and don't know anyone. We plan to go back up to the bluff in the morning and question all the neighbors. We'll try to find out who is home during the day."

~~~

In the Milligan household, the family had finished their dinner, but everyone still sat around the table chatting. Doug told a bit about what was happening with the missing woman, Geneva Portman, but he admitted they hadn't really gotten very far.

Stacey added the information she'd heard from Mrs. Portman's friends hadn't helped much. "I'd hoped something would come of her old lover, Roger Endicott."

Beth sighed. "At least, you two get to be out and see people. You have no idea how boring it is just sitting here at home all the time." Despite being home, Beth had new colorful streaks in her hair: red, blue, purple, and green.

She wore a long, white, man's shirt that had once belonged to her father over a pair of rainbow-patterned tights.

Doug guessed she felt she needed to be her usual self while doing her schoolwork online since her classmates and teacher could see her. "Hey, at least you have Kayla to keep you company."

Beth gave Kayla a quick hug. "I wouldn't survive without her."

"I feel the same." Kayla had tied a long blue-green scarf around her blonde curls. The end of the scarf trailed down over the back of her overall shorts. She wore a short-sleeved blouse with peace signs all over it.

"Couldn't we take a walk down to the beach? We really need the exercise." Beth used a most pleading expression.

Stacey glanced at Doug.

He guessed she might think it would be okay. But what if the girls ran into someone who had the virus? "What do you think, Stacey? Should we let them?"

"Please, please." Beth focused on Stacey.

"If they keep their masks on and only go to the beach and back." Stacey didn't sound all that enthusiastic.

Both girls jumped up from the table and ran upstairs to Beth's bedroom.

"Maybe it isn't such a good idea." Doug was glad Davey was at his grandparents so he didn't have to contend with him wanting to go somewhere, too.

"Too late. They're getting ready. We'll have to trust them to use good sense while they're out there."

When the girls came downstairs, they both had their masks in their hands and had donned sweatshirts with hoodies.

Beth rushed to her parents and kissed both of them on the cheek. "Thank you. Thank you."

Both girls dashed toward the front door while they put on their masks.

"Don't stay away for more than two hours." Stacey called after them.

"Two hours? That seems like an awfully long time." Doug frowned.

"It's going to take twenty minutes to a half hour to get to the beach on foot, and they'll want to spend some time at the ocean. Two hours is about right."

Doug sighed. "Whatever you say, though I'm not sure this is such a good idea."

~~~

Since COVID-19, in Rocky Bluff the evening hours had mostly been quiet. People even seemed to be obeying the traffic laws. Though the bigger cities had experienced some destructive demonstrations against law enforcement, nothing similar had happened in Rocky Bluff.

After supper, Ryan Strickland and his wife, Barbara, had watched the evening news together, something they usually did, especially now while trying to find out any news about the coronavirus.

Appalled by what he'd seen on the news about happenings in places like Seattle and Portland, Ryan Strickland turned off the TV. "People have gone nuts. No matter what the police did wrong, tearing down their own neighborhoods and ransacking stores doesn't solve anything."

The boys were all in their bedrooms, and from the sounds coming down the hallway, at least two of them were involved with a lively computer game. Since Tony, the oldest of Barbara's sons, had revealed he had a girlfriend in Fresno, they now knew he spent nearly as much time

FaceTiming with her as doing his studies on the computer. As yet, they'd not been told much about his new love.

Keeping their daughter, Angel, safe was Barbara's biggest concern. Because their daughter had Down syndrome, she was in the compromised category.

Watching his daughter always improved Ryan's mood. She played with toys on the carpet in front of them. Ryan thought her the prettiest toddler he'd ever seen. She smiled nearly all the time. She'd inherited her mother's curly hair. She looked and acted in the peak of health.

Though he didn't take his gaze from Angel, he could hear the boisterous sounds from the bedroom. "I'm surprised we haven't had more problems with the boys wanting to go out."

Barbara laughed. "Letting them play video games as long as they want after their schoolwork is done has helped. And though I didn't expect it, the boys have really enjoyed working in the garden."

At the beginning of the COVID crisis, Barbara suggested the boys should create a vegetable garden in the backyard. Ryan had taken them to the garden department of one of the big stores in Ventura where they'd purchased all their supplies and plants. He'd warned them the garden was their responsibility because it wasn't anything he knew about. They'd done a great job, and the family had already been eating much of what they'd grown, with the promise of much more to come.

Barbara, who'd started crocheting what she said would be an afghan, pulled yarn and her crochet hook from a large colorful bag. "I've had lots of phone calls from the other wives."

"What are they yakking about now?" Ryan knew the police wives had an active phone network.

"Oh, all kinds of theories about what's going on."

"Like what?"

"Everything from we're being lied to and the disease isn't nearly as bad as they say, to it's far worse than we're being told, it's really germ warfare, and many of us will die before it's over." Barbara's fingers skillfully maneuvered the crochet hook through the yarn.

"I hear the same stuff at work."

"Half don't like wearing the masks and call it another way for the government to control us."

"The masks are a pain to wear, and I'm not sure how much protection they afford. But I suppose a little bit is better than nothing."

"I've been telling people washing your hands really good is something we should have been doing all along. That's what Abel's wife told me, and she thinks we should wear masks whenever we're out in public. She also said they have quite a few cases of the virus at the hospital, some serious."

He'd heard a lot of the same from Abel. "Since she's a nurse, she knows what she's talking about."

Barbara's fingers stilled for a moment. "Be honest with me, Ryan. Do you think we'll have any riots here in Rocky Bluff?"

There was no way he could predict the future. Since he'd heard some rioters were being paid to bring havoc to places where they didn't live, he couldn't honestly tell his wife it wouldn't happen in their town. "We're so small, I don't think anyone will bother with us."

"I hope not. I know all the businesses are struggling. We don't need any extra trouble."

"Let's change the subject. I have to hear all this stuff at work, too."

"Why don't you tell me what's going on at work? Any interesting cases?" Her fingers flew as she worked the crochet hook through the yarn.

He brought her up-to-date on the missing woman and what little he knew about the garage burglary. He didn't mention the house fire and the dead family.

Chapter 12

The girls had only been gone about a half hour when the Staci's cellphone rang.

Doug's eyes flew open. "Don't tell me they're in trouble already."

Stacey glanced at the phone. "It's my mother." She answered, "Hi, Mom."

At the sound of Clara's voice Stacey knew something was wrong. "I'm sorry but your father is bringing Davey home."

"Why? Did he do something wrong?"

"Heavens no. Davey's perfect, and we want him to stay that way. I'm not feeling well, and neither is your father. To be on the safe side, we're going to isolate ourselves."

"What do you mean, you're not feeling well?"

"I woke up with a sore throat and blamed it on snoring. It happens to me sometimes. But I've gargled with salt water, drank what seems like a gallon of tea with honey, and it's not getting better. I think I might have a temperature, too."

"Oh, Mom. You should call the doctor."

"I will if I'm not better in the morning. Keep an eye on Davey. I'll feel dreadful if I've given him something."

By the time Clara had hung up, Davey burst through the door. "Grammy's sick."

Stacey's father only came in far enough to deposit a suitcase. "Here are Davey's clothes. I need to get back home to your mother."

Davey ran to Doug and hugged him. "I'm glad to be home."

"We're glad to have you home." Doug peered over Davey's head at Stacey. "How're we going to work this?"

"We'll have to rely on Beth and Kayla to keep an eye on Davey."

"What about your folks?"

Stacey shrugged. "Mom has to be feeling really bad to send Davey home."

"Do you think they have the virus?"

"I hope not. If so, Davey's been exposed, and we all could be, too."

"With the jobs we have, we're exposed all the time. No point in worrying about it."

Stacey couldn't help but worry. If her parents had the virus, they'd all been exposed. "Mom said she'd go to the doctor tomorrow. I hope they both do."

Their concern about their folks and Davey took their minds off Beth and Kayla.

~~~

Chief Chandra Taylor poured herself a second glass of wine and settled down on her big couch in front of the TV. After eating her dinner, she'd taken a long bath, changed into nightgown and robe, planning to have a restful evening. No TV news for her. She'd find a soothing romance to watch.

While she checked through the movies offered on Netflix, her cellphone rang. Her first thought was not to answer, but being the chief of police, she couldn't do that. She glanced at the caller ID. Devon Duvall.

Her heart thumped. "Yes, Devon, how may I help you?"

"Have you time to talk?"

"I do."

"Some of the council members have been calling me. They want me to put in some kind of proclamation that everyone in Rocky Bluff must wear a mask when in public. And they want there to be some kind of fine for anyone caught without a mask."

"What did you tell them?"

"I don't want to do any such thing." He paused. "They plan on voting on it at the next council meeting."

"You can tell them for me the police department doesn't have time to enforce such a law or proclamation or whatever they want to call it." *Such foolishness.* "Don't those silly council members realize that the police department has more important duties—like keeping them safe."

"They also want to allow outdoor dining, using patios and parking lots."

She thought for a moment. "I don't see anything wrong with that idea."

"Patrons would have to wear masks."

This comment struck her as funny as she pictured folks lifting up masks in order to eat. She laughed. "Not when they're eating."

"Of course not, but when they arrive and wait to be seated."

"Sounds kind of silly, but a lot of what's going on is a bit silly."

Devon cleared his throat. "I'm not sure what you mean." He sounded a bit offended.

"Oh, I have to laugh when I see people driving around by themselves wearing a mask. Or wearing gloves and touching everything, but not changing and putting on new gloves. Washing hands properly and often is probably far more effective."

This time he took a deep breath. "Let's change the subject. Any more news about outside demonstrators coming to Rocky Bluff?"

"Nothing tangible, but we're monitoring the Internet sites closely. Don't worry. As soon as we know about any such movement, we'll be on it."

"I sure hope so."

"Have faith in us, Devon. We're small but mighty." She made sure to sound positive, but deep down she wondered how effective her few men and women would be against an angry crowd.

"I can hardly wait for life to return to normal. I'd like to spend more time with you, and not to discuss city problems."

Chandra suspected it might be far off. In the beginning, she'd wondered if Devon would become a major romantic interest in her life. Now, it didn't look like anything would develop between the two of them. Something always got in the way.

~ ~ ~

Gordon Butler started his evening shift not expecting to have much to do. He drove around the quiet streets. He'd never seen them so empty.

Though he hadn't been pleased about his wife being the training officer for the new hire, it sounded like Patrick O'Brien might be an all right guy. And he was married, so Gordon didn't have to worry about him hitting on his wife. Since Lizette had pointed out the last new guy, the one Gordon trained, didn't act right toward women, he'd been worried about this new trainee.

What really bothered him was that the chief had asked Lizette rather than him to be the training officer this time. Hadn't he done a good enough job? Though it took a while for him to realize the guy was doing things he shouldn't, he'd reported him immediately.

Silly to keep thinking about it. He'd done the job of training officer to the best of his ability. Though things had gotten so much better for him since he married Lizette, he would never forget how many years he'd been the brunt of everyone's jokes. Despite the fact he'd always performed by the book, things often didn't turn out the way he'd planned.

Oh, he had plenty of friends on the department. Doug and Stacey Milligan were at the top of the list. They'd even provided their home for his and Lizette's wedding.

Time to put the bad memories behind him. Lizette had certainly encouraged him to do it many times. He knew a lot of his fellow cops had been amazed when Lizette agreed to marry him, but none more than he. He knew he hadn't impressed her when they met, but when he'd risked his life to save hers, she'd viewed him in a different manner.

Gordon made his final loop around the residential district he was assigned to when his radio came to life. He was to join other officers to investigate a disturbance at the beach.

Before he'd even parked his car, even though the fog had rolled in, he could see smoke rising on the other side of the dunes.

Even during normal times, bonfires weren't allowed on the beach, though people often tried to get by with smaller fires. From the smoke he could see, Gordon knew this wasn't a small fire.

Chapter 13

Doug glanced at his watch. "The girls have been gone a long time."

"Don't worry. This is the first time they've been on their own." Stacey had been in the kitchen baking cookies for tomorrow's lunches. "Let them enjoy themselves. They don't know they're going to have to take care of Davey yet."

Doug paced from the dining room to the kitchen. "If they don't show up within the next half hour, I'm going to look for them."

"Whatever you think you have to do." Stacey passed him on her way to the bedroom. "I think I'll take a shower while the stew in simmering."

Doug knew his wife's biggest concern was her parents' health. She was probably right about the girls. They were probably taking advantage of the situation. He knew he'd have done the same thing when he was their age, and likely much more. But darn it, they'd done so well with Beth since she'd come to live with them. He didn't want anything to spoil it now. Beth's mother, his ex-wife, always threw a fit when anything went wrong concerning Beth. And of course, there was the added responsibility of Kyla, the mayor's daughter. Right now, he wished he hadn't agreed to let her come to stay with Beth.

The minutes dragged by.

He stepped out on the front porch and looked down the street, one way and then the other. Fog swirled up from the ocean making the street lights dim. He couldn't see all the way to the corner. The smell of smoke, almost like a campfire floated in, along with the damp scent of the ocean. *Not another fire.*

Back in the house, he used his cellphone to call the department and asked for the sergeant on duty.

Abel Navarro answered. "What's up, Milligan?"

"That's what I called to ask you. What's going on? I can smell smoke."

"A disturbance at the beach. A bonfire. Officers have responded, but I haven't gotten a report yet."

"Thanks." Doug disconnected before Abel could ask him anything.

Outside the bathroom door, he heard the shower. He poked his head in the room. "Davey's watching a movie on TV. I'm going to find the girls."

He grabbed his jacket and his car keys and headed out.

~~~

Never easy to walk on the beach with shoes on. Gordon hurried as fast as possible in the direction of a huge bonfire. One of the other cops who'd responded plowed along ahead, the beam of his flashlight falling on ruffled sand.

Ahead of the light, dark shapes moved around the outside of the flames.

Someone shouted, "It's the cops."

The dark shapes scattered. Some came right in Gordon's direction. "Halt. Police." What he should do now he was uncertain about. He certainly wasn't going to shoot or even use his night stick. No one stopped.

One of those fleeing, nearly ran into Gordon, and he grabbed an arm.

Surprisingly the person stopped. "Oh, no. It's you."

Gordon shone his flashlight in the person's face. Though a hoodie had been pulled down and almost covered her eyes, he recognized the teen immediately. "You're Detective Milligan's daughter."

"Yes, sir." She bowed her head.

"What's going on here?"

"Some kids decided to have a bonfire. My friend and I haven't been down here long and weren't anywhere near the fire. My dad let us walk down here to see the ocean."

"You know it's illegal to have a fire on the beach."

"We didn't build it. We didn't even know anyone was going to do it."

Another girl stood right behind Beth Milligan. Gordon recognized her, too: the mayor's daughter.

A couple of the other officers had rounded up a few other kids and were marching them toward the parking lot.

"Couldn't you just let us go home?" Beth asked. "We didn't do anything wrong."

"The first thing I have to do is get the fire department here to put out the fire."

Someone else must've called because sirens screamed in the distance.

"Okay, let's head toward my car and sort this out."

Both girls walked beside him, heads down. He didn't hang on to either one as he felt sure they wouldn't run. After all, he knew who they were.

"How come you kids don't have on masks? I might not have recognized you if your faces had been covered."

Beth plodded along beside him. "We wore them down here, but the whole idea was to see and smell the ocean."

Kayla spoke up. "We're been cooped up for months. It's the first time Beth's folks let us go out."

"And it'll probably be the last time." Beth spoke so softly Gordon could hardly hear her.

Fire personnel appeared out of the fog and galloped toward the bonfire. The yellow stripes on their turnout gear seemed to glow as they ran. Some carried shovels, and several pulled a fire hose.

Blurred shapes of young people darted down the beach, some toward the street disappearing into the fog, with a couple of officers in pursuit. The sand muffled all the sound of footfalls. It was impossible to understand most of the words being shouted.

As sand was scooped onto the flames, sparks rose and disappeared into the mist. Water sprayed, and the fire diminished and sizzled

Beth turned back. "It was pretty awesome."

"Glad we got to see it even if we do get in trouble."

"Keep moving. I'm anxious to get you girls home to your folks." Gordon stepped up his pace. Beth and Kayla trudged along beside him.

When they'd almost reached his patrol car, an SUV pulled into the crowded parking lot.

Beth stopped. "Uh, oh. That looks like my dad's car."

~ ~ ~

Doug braked and leapt from the driver's seat, and left the door open. He'd already spotted the girls walking on either side of Gordon Butler. Even before he reached them, he began hollering questions. "What's going on? What did you do? Are you taking them to the station?"

By the time he reached them, Gordon held up a hand. "Whoa. Everything's okay. I was going to take the girls home. They aren't in any trouble."

"Then what's the fire department doing here? Who are all these kids? Why are officers here?"

Beth stepped closer to Doug. "He's right, Dad. Listen to him. We didn't have anything to do with the bonfire."

Bonfire explained the fire department. "Okay, then what were you doing? You know better than to hang out with other kids right now."

"We came to the beach like we said, but we took a long time getting here. We walked down Valley Boulevard and checked things out first. When we reached the beach, the bonfire was already burning. We went all the way down to the water because it was what we came to see. We didn't get close to any of the other kids."

Kayla chimed in. "That's right. I don't think anyone even knew we were there."

"Both of you, get in the car. I need to let Stacey know you're both safe." He pulled his cellphone from his pocket. "Thanks, Gordon."

"I'm pretty sure they're telling the truth. They weren't near the fire when I spotted them."

"Great." He called home. "Hi, Stacey. I'm bringing the girls home now. They're fine." Phone back in his pocket, he turned to Gordon. "Really, thanks, man. We gave them permission to walk down here, but they were gone a long time. You're sure they weren't doing anything wrong?"

"Naw. They weren't even a part of the other group. And except for building the bonfire, I don't think the other kids were up to anything more than maybe having a few beers. I can understand all of them wanting to get out for a while."

"Thanks again." Doug headed back to the SUV. He didn't have any idea what he was going to say to the girls, if anything. They'd sure had him worried, but if Gordon was right and they hadn't done anything wrong, he should merely be happy they were safe. He wondered how they'd feel about the fact they had a new job, taking care of Davey.

Chapter 14

When the girls entered the house, both with their heads down, Stacey knew they expected her to admonish them. However, she was delighted to see they were okay. She threw her arms around Beth and Kayla and hugged them tight. "Oh, I'm so glad you're home. I couldn't help worrying."

Doug stood behind them, a confused expression on his face. "I found them at the beach. The police and the fire department were there because someone had built a huge bonfire."

"We didn't have anything to do with the bonfire." Beth didn't try to pull away from Stacey's embrace.

Kayla took a step back. "We didn't even talk to anyone except for Officer Butler."

Stacey glanced at Doug.

"Gordon spotted the girls and was planning to bring them home."

"I'm sure you must be cold. I've got hot chocolate on the stove plus cookies. Let's go in the kitchen. I have something very important to tell you." Stacey led the way.

She didn't speak again until she'd poured each of the girls a mug of the hot drink and popped a marshmallow on top of each one. She gave Doug a cup of coffee.

When everyone was around the table, she said. "It's not good news. Both of my parents are sick. They haven't been tested yet, but they're going to the doctor tomorrow. What this means for you two is I'm going to need you to take care of Davey. He's going to need help with his schoolwork. I know both of you are busy with your own, but neither of us can take time off right now."

"How sick are your folks?" Beth stirred the melting marshmallow in her cup. "Since we had dinner over there, if she has the virus doesn't it mean we were all exposed?"

"We don't know yet if she has it. In any case, the three of you'll stay home no matter how this turns out. We'll speak to the chief and see what she wants us to do."

Doug spoke in a rush. "I didn't have dinner with them on Sunday."

"But you've been around all of us." Stacey put the bag of marshmallows on the table. "Help yourselves."

Kayla plopped two more marshmallows into her cup. "My mom used to make hot chocolate like this. She always said we had chocolate with our marshmallows."

Doug stood. "I'll call Chief Taylor right now. I can't imagine she'll want me to stay out with so much going on."

~~~

Chief Taylor wasn't at all happy when she heard the Milligans' news. "Both of you?" She thought for a minute. *Her lead detective and one of her best officers out of commission for two weeks.* There was no way she could let them come in.

"Yes, chief. The big problem is our son has been staying with my in-laws, and now he's home with us. Plus, Stacey and the girls were with my in-laws on Sunday."

"Fourteen days off."

"We don't even know if my in-laws have the virus."

"We can't take a chance. If they test negative, then you can come back to work."

Doug sounded disheartened. "I'll do whatever I can from here."

"Let Zachary know he's on his own." She disconnected. *Crap. The missing woman case, the dead family in the house fire, and only one detective to investigate. And there was always the threat of outsiders coming in to cause problems.*

She wondered if it was too late to call Devon. The fact that the news affected his daughter too convinced her.

"Hey, Chandra, what's going on?"

"Have the Milligans contacted you yet?"

"No, but Kayla did. Are you calling about the bonfire at the beach?"

"What does the bonfire have to do with Kayla?"

"Seems she and the Milligans' daughter were down there."

"Hadn't heard about that yet. Did they have anything to do with the fire?"

"Kayla says not, and I believe her. Detective Milligan let the girls take a walk to the beach. When they got there, the fire was already going strong."

Of course, Devon would believe his daughter. To be honest, Chandra believed her, too. She wasn't the kind of girl to lie about something like that. "Both the Milligans will be out of commission for at least fourteen days because they've possibly been exposed to the virus. And that's if they don't end up testing positive themselves. Really leaves me short-handed."

"I thought the virus had kind of kept a lid on crime."

"Yes, as long as we don't get any outsiders coming in to demonstrate like we talked about." She guessed Devon hadn't grasped the fact Kayla might have been exposed to the virus, too. "Devon, your daughter has been exposed to the virus right along the Milligans."

He didn't say anything for a long moment. "Of course. Kayla's living with them. I guess I'll have to hope for the best. She didn't even mention this to me."

"I don't think they found out until later today. That's why I'll be short-handed."

"How can I help you?"

"Frankly, I don't know. What I'm thinking right now is if we do hear about some troublemakers planning something, I'll need to get some outside help. I'm sure you'd agree to that."

"Of course."

She was about to tell him goodbye, but he spoke again. "How about stopping by for breakfast before you go to work? I'm not much of a cook. The one thing I'm really good at is making a great omelet. I have a loaf of that wonderful sourdough from the bakery in the market, too. What do you say? We don't have a chance to see much of each other these days."

Though she knew she should go in early, she wanted to see Devon as much as he seemed to want to see her. And she had to eat, didn't she?

"Yes, I'd like that."

"I'd like that, but since you'll be so busy, I'll bring the food."

~~~

Doug called Felix at seven a.m.

"Hey, Milligan, what's up?"

"Have some bad news, partner."

"Yeah? What?"

He explained the situation, ending with, "It means I have to stay home for fourteen days."

"Sorry to hear about your in-laws. What do you want me to do first?"

"See if you can get any information from the relator handling the sale of Roger Endicott's house. I hope she helped him find a new place. If you get an address, check it out. And as long as I'm home, I'll call the ME's office and see what they can tell me about their findings on the Barberick family's remains. If anything else comes up I can handle from home, let me know."

Doug could hear Wendy in the background asking questions. He hoped she wouldn't freak out when she heard what was going on. Felix had complained about how paranoid his wife was about the virus.

"Okay, Milligan, I'll call you with any information as soon as I get it."

Since Doug had made his call while sitting at the kitchen table, he watched Stacey whip up a big batch of pancakes. Even though they were all home, since all the kids had schoolwork, they were sticking to their usual schedule.

"Too bad we can't pack up and go somewhere." Doug got up and poured himself another cup of coffee.

"We can't even go to the store. Quarantine means staying at home away from other people. Good thing I really stocked up when I shopped on Saturday."

"We can always have stuff delivered if we run out."

"I think we'll be okay."

Stacey's phone rang. "My father." She answered, "Hi, Dad."

She listened, and her face gathered into a frown. "Should I come? Oh, I forgot. I can't. Call me the minute you know something."

Doug carried his full cup to the table. "I can tell by your expression it's not good news."

"No, it isn't. Mom's being admitted to the hospital. They're sending Dad home. They've both been tested, but it takes time to get the results. No one can go to see her." Stacey wiped tears from her eyes. "We'll have to be tested, too."

"We'll get it done." What filled his thoughts were ways he could help their investigation of the missing woman case. So much time had gone by. He now feared for Mrs. Portman's life.

Chapter 15

Wendy wasn't at all happy when she heard what Milligan's phone call had been about. "You two spend all of your time together—the majority of it cooped up in a car, breathing each other's air. And I know you don't wear your masks when you're driving around."

She was right about the masks. "I'll get tested right away, but I can't stay home." Felix drank the rest of the second cup of coffee his wife had poured him.

Ruby, a lovely combination of her parents' genes, sat at the table with them, crunching away at a bowl of Cheerios, oblivious to the tense discussion.

"If you test positive, I don't know what we'll do. We'll all have to be quarantined."

"Don't worry about it yet. I'll be extra careful. In fact, I'll disinfect the car we usually drive."

"Better yet, drive your own car for the next few days until we know if Milligan or his family test positive." She was quiet even longer. "Maybe you should get a hotel room."

"Wait a minute, Wendy. I'm not getting a hotel room. I'll take all the precautions necessary, but if I've been exposed to anything, you have, too."

Wendy's face pulled into a gigantic frown, and tears poured down her cheeks.

"Oh, for Pete's sake, Wendy." He jumped up from his chair and scooped his wife out of hers. He gave her a huge hug. "Aw, honey, don't cry. I hate to see you cry."

Ruby gazed up at them, her face puckered, too.

"Now you've got Ruby started for nothing." Felix kissed Wendy on the forehead and released her.

He reached toward Ruby just as his mother came into the kitchen. He couldn't see her expression because it was hidden by her mask. "What on earth is going on in here?"

"I'm going to let Wendy explain. I can't be late for work." He grabbed his jacket off his chair and rushed toward the door. The quicker he could escape, the better. He did not want to be interrogated by his mother.

~~~

Devon opened his front door just as Chandra parked her car in front of his house. He had a dishtowel tied around the waist of his light-blue striped shirt, and dark navy trousers. His smile was huge.

Chandra's heart jumped. What a great way to start what she knew would be a difficult day. Out of the car, she hurried toward his open arms.

Devon hugged her tightly and kissed her forehead. "I'm so glad to see you."

When he released her, he said, "Come right in, I've already dished up our plates, and the coffee is poured. I knew you'd be in a hurry."

Though she hadn't taken a lot of time to choose her clothing for the day, she was happy she'd picked her most comfortable jacket and pants outfit. It also fit her the best. The dark gray set off the brightly patterned orange, red, yellow, and white blouse she wore under the nicely-shaped jacket.

"Oh, my, that looks delicious." Chandra scooted into the chair Devon held for her.

"I hope you like it. Dig in."

The fluffy folded omelet contained bits of bacon, tomatoes, mushrooms, and cheddar cheese, with two pieces of buttered sourdough toast at the top of the plate.

After her first bite, Chandra closed her eyes. "Yummy." It was her last comment until the omelet was gone and all but a half piece of toast. "Perfect way to start the day. Thank you for doing this, Devon."

"Have another cup of coffee." Devon already held the coffee pot in his hand.

Chandra glanced at her watch. "I have time for half a cup."

"We should do this more often." Devon sat down again and studied her.

"Have breakfast together?"

"Yes, and other meals, too." He reached out and grasped her hand. "We need to plan time together."

"I'd like that. But now I have to get moving. Today will be difficult."

"If you want to talk later, give me a call." His dark eyes seemed to be pleading.

"Or, since your daughter isn't here, you could come to my house this evening. I'm not much of a cook, but I can pick up some Mexican food on the way home. I can call first so you'll know when to come." It would be the first time he'd been to her house.

"I'd like that."

~~~

When Lizette arrived at the police station, she had a message to see Chief Taylor. *What now?* Any time the chief requested Lizette's presence, she felt a sense of dread. Taking a deep breath and smoothing her uniform shirt to make sure it was tucked in, she knocked on the chief's inner office door.

A loud, "Come in," started Lizette's heart pumping. For goodness sake, she hadn't done anything wrong. Why was she so nervous?

Chief Taylor beamed at Lizette. Her expression was nearly as sunny as the yellow in the brightly colored blouse she wore. Lizette relaxed. "You wanted to see me, ma'am?"

"Sit, please."

Lizette slid into a chair in front of the desk and waited.

The chief folded her hands "How are things going with you and your trainee?"

"Good."

"I heard you were called to a burglary. Have you gotten anywhere on it?"

"Not yet, but Patrick, I mean Officer O'Brien, had a similar case where he worked before. The guilty party was someone in the neighborhood, and we suspect it might be the same with this case."

"Sounds like you might need to do some surveillance."

"Yes, ma'am. That was our plan."

"We are going to be pretty short-handed for the next ten days."

The department had been short-handed for as long as Lizette had been there. "Yes, ma'am."

"Detective Milligan and Officer Milligan have both been exposed to the virus, which means they're off work as of now."

"Oh, no. I hadn't heard."

"So, I can't really let the two of you spend all your time watching a neighborhood. What I wondered is how much longer will it be before O'Brien is ready to be on his own?"

"He's experienced and seems competent. The only problem is I haven't had a chance to show him all of Rocky Bluff yet."

"Do you think you could accomplish it today?"

"Yes, ma'am."

~~~

Patrick seemed disappointed when Lizette told him the news.

She was surprised. "I thought you'd be thankful to be on your own."

"I'd hoped we could catch whoever burglarized the garage. My hunch is whoever it was will do it again and probably fairly soon. Plus, I still have lots of questions."

"I'm going to show you the rest of the Rocky Bluff area today. You'll also have GPS in all of the patrol cars to help you find an address. Ask as many questions as you like while we're patrolling today. You have my phone number. You can call me anytime." Her plan was to take him under the freeway and up to the hillside area where the ranches and orange groves were.

Once they'd checked out a car and began driving, Patrick asked, "Do you think Rocky Bluff will have any trouble from any of the protest groups?"

"I hope not, but I'm sure the chief is concerned about it since we're so short of manpower."

"My wife was asking me if I'd heard anything. She's been keeping up with all the reports from the cities around us."

"I think we're too small for anyone to bother with us."

"Maybe, but it would be pretty easy for even a small group to come in here and really wreak havoc."

"Chief Taylor is smart. I'm sure she's considered the possibility and has some sort of plan in place. I know she has our computer guy monitoring all the activity and threats via the Internet."

Once they were in the car, seat belted, and ready to go, Lizette asked, "Do you think you can find all the places I've shown you so far?"

"Yes, I do."

She headed toward the 101. "The highway bisects Rocky Bluff. Once we go under the overpass, it's like we're in a different place."

"I remember."

Rocky Bluff consisted of several different areas. The business section ran along and around the main street. The main residential area ran from the beach up the sloping hills to the freeway. The southernmost part had the restaurant, the abandoned pier, the acreage, which had once held an abandoned warehouse, and ended with the campground. The bluff held all the expensive homes. The other side of the highway had a totally different atmosphere than the beach side, much like going into the countryside.

~~~

Felix Zachary made two phone calls. When he'd finished, he contacted Doug Milligan. "Hey, how're you feeling?"

"I'm fine. Not happy about having to stay home. What's happening?"

"Went ahead and contacted the ME's office. They have nothing for us yet. Got hold of the real estate lady who sold Endicott's house. He bought another. It's in the hills above Santa Barbara. Thought I'd take a run up there and check it out."

"I wish I could go with you."

"I do too, but Wendy would throw a fit."

"Anything else going on?"

"Butler's wife and the new recruit caught a garage burglary up in the bluffs. They think it's probably someone who lives up there, but right now, we're so shorthanded, they can't do any surveillance in the area."

"A crazy thought popped into my head. Let me run it by you." Milligan sounded excited.

Chapter 16

Even though Felix had agreed that Doug's idea would work, he knew he should discuss it with Chief Taylor to get her permission, and Lizette Butler, too.

Doug used his cellphone to call the station, and asked for the chief.

She answered quickly. "Not showing signs of the virus, I hope."

"No, nothing like that. I've had an idea I wanted to run by you."

"What?"

"I heard about the garage burglary. Since I can't work in my usual capacity, I thought I could do surveillance in the neighborhood. Sitting in my car, no contact with anyone. What do you think?"

Taylor took a minute before she answered. "If you want to, I don't see why not. I'll have Officer Butler get in touch with you to give you the details."

"Great." He disconnected.

He'd made his phone calls at the kitchen table while Stacey prepared breakfast. When he was done, she turned from the stove and stared at him with a quizzical expression.

"She agreed? I'm surprised."

"Hey, we're so shorthanded she's probably glad for any help."

"What happens if you see something? You can't arrest anyone right now. If the person got sick, they'd no doubt sue the city."

"No, I won't arrest anyone, but I can take photographs, see what the M.O. is, and one of the cops on duty can do the arresting. I'll call Lizette Butler and let her and the rookie take care of it."

Stacey pouted. "I'm jealous."

"Don't be. Sitting in a car all day is boring. I might not see anything worthwhile. Besides, you get to be home with the kids."

"Speaking of kids, how about letting them all know breakfast is ready." She began dishing up plates of scrambled eggs with bits of tomato and onions, smothered with cheese. A tray of steaming biscuits already sat on the table, along with a platter of crispy bacon. He was definitely going to eat before he left.

He still had to wait for Butler to call so he could find out the details of the burglary case.

~~~

Before the family finished eating, Stacey received a call on her cellphone. Ordinarily, she wouldn't have answered during a meal, but the ID said it was from her mother. She left the kitchen and went into the living room. "How are you doing, Mom?"

"Not so good. I'm having trouble breathing. The doctor wants to put me on a ventilator, and I don't want that. I'd rather go on to heaven."

Tears filled Stacey's eyes. "Oh, Mom, don't say that. Let the doctors do whatever they need to do."

"I'm not sure the doctors have any idea what they should be doing to treat this illness. Some I've heard about who went on a ventilator didn't do well. I'd rather not go through what I've heard it's like to be on a ventilator."

"Mom, please. I don't want to lose you." Stacey's tears flowed.

"I'm not ready to die, either." She coughed. "I have something I want you to do. Call Reverend Cookmeyer and all my friends at church. Ask them to pray for me."

"I'll do it right away. I love you, Mom. I'll get the kids to pray, too."

"Let your father know, too. It's hard not being able to see him. My battery is getting low so I have to go. Tell everyone I love them." She disconnected.

Stacey sobbed quietly until she was able to pull herself together. After wiping her eyes, she returned to the kitchen.

Everyone stared at her.

Doug said, "You've been crying, and I can tell by your expression it wasn't good news."

"No, it wasn't. Mom says they want to put her on a ventilator. She said she'd rather go to heaven."

Davey's eyes grew large. "Is Grandma going to die?"

"Hush, don't say that." Beth put her arm around Davey.

Doug spoke firmly. "I'm sure she'll be all right."

Stacey was glad Doug had tried to reassure Davey, even though she shared her son's concern.

She slumped back in her chair. "She wants me to call Reverend Cookmeyer and all her friends at church and ask for prayer."

Kayla raised her hand. "Your mom has been great to me. Why don't we all pray for her now?"

Stacey was surprised when Doug reached out and took her hand. "Let's join hands and pray for her right now." He glanced at Stacey. "Will you do the honors?"

She bowed her head and the others followed. "Lord in heaven, we lift up my mother to you. We ask for speedy and complete healing. We put her into your hands, Lord.

We know you are the great physician. I pray this in your Son's name, Amen."

Everyone joined in the amen.

Beth started clearing the table. "Kayla and I will clean up the kitchen so you can get busy making phone calls."

Davey stuffed a last piece of toast in his mouth and picked up his own plate. "I'll help, too."

"Thanks, kids." Stacey took her cellphone into the living room and called Reverend Cookmeyer first.

~~~

It wasn't long before Doug received the call he waited for.

"Hey, Detective Milligan, how are you and your wife?" It was Lizette Butler.

"Neither of us has any symptoms. I'm sure we'll be fine."

"Glad to hear it. The chief says you want to help with the burglary case. It would be a great if you could because she wants O'Brien and me back on patrol duty." Officer Butler sounded pleased.

"I might as well be sitting in the neighborhood as here at home. Give me the address where the burglary took place and anything else you know."

She told him the location. "My trainee had a similar experience with a garage burglary where he worked before. A neighbor watched the owner's comings and goings. In the case he worked on, the neighbor followed the victim to work, used a shim to get in the passenger door, reached in to take the garage door remote, closed the door but left it unlocked. Back at the homeowner's home, he used the remote. Once the garage was open, the burglar loaded up what he wanted to steal. Once he was finished, he took the opener back to the victim's car and locked the door."

"Slick. Did you have a chance to talk to any of the neighbors to see if anyone saw anything?"

"No. We didn't have time. Plus, according to the victim, everyone in the neighborhood works."

Questioning neighbors wasn't something he could do. "I'm surprised the victim didn't have some kind of security system especially since they live up there on the bluff."

"We were, too, but she said they hadn't lived there long and hadn't gotten around to it."

"If all of the neighbors are away at work, none of them may be guilty. I'm not sure I'll find anything out, but it's worth a try."

"Thanks for doing this."

He told Stacey where he was going and what he was going to do, she merely nodded because she was on the phone.

He went into the kitchen where the girls were busy loading the dishwasher. "I'm going to be gone most of the day."

Beth glanced at him. "We heard."

Kayla gave him a thumbs up.

"Be sure and do whatever you have to do for school. Help Davey if he needs it."

"Don't worry, Dad, we'll do what we're supposed to."

"Don't give your mother any trouble. She's really upset."

Beth rolled her eyes. "We know, Dad. Go take care of your business."

~ ~ ~

Stacey finished making her calls to the minister and each of her mother's friends. She thought a moment, then decided to contact the hospital. It took a long time for them to answer.

"I'd like to speak with Maria Navarro, please."

"One moment."

If Abel's wife was working, maybe she could get some details from about her mother's condition.

It took even longer before Maria came on the line. "This is Nurse Navarro."

"Maria, it's Stacey Milligan. I have a favor to ask. My mom, Clara Osborne, is there. Could you check and see how she's doing?"

"I planned on calling you later. I saw she'd been placed in ICU. She's very sick, Stacey."

"Mom called me and said the doctor wants to put her on a ventilator, but she doesn't want that. She said she'd rather die and go to heaven."

"It doesn't matter what she wants. The doctor has to do whatever it takes to try and save her life."

Stacey wasn't sure whether if what she heard was good or not. "Thank you, Maria. Could you keep me posted?"

After she hung up, Stacey wondered what else she could do.

Chapter 17

Stacey remembered one other person she knew who had a lot of faith and believed in the power of prayer: Ryan Strickland's wife, Barbara, a devout Catholic.

She answered the phone almost immediately. "Hi, Stacey, I heard that you and your whole family have been exposed to this dreadful virus. How are you feeling?"

"So far, none of us have any symptoms."

"Good. Is there something I can do for you?"

"Yes, there is. My mother is the one who's sick. She's in the hospital now."

"Oh no. I'll pray for her."

"That's exactly what I was going to ask you to do."

"I'll contact everyone I know."

"Wonderful."

"I'll pray for you and your family, too. I know this has to be so difficult."

"It is. Thank you, Barbara."

~~~

Though fog had been rolling in from the ocean when Doug left his house, the mist had burned away on the bluff. Or maybe it hadn't even come up this far. No wonder people liked living up here.

The neighborhood on the bluff where the garage burglary had taken place was well-kept, and the houses all looked expensive. Doug drove slowly down the block. As had been reported, it didn't look as though anyone on either side of the street was home.

He decided to park at the far end of the block. He'd brought some water and snacks to fortify himself. He settled down to the boring job of watching this part of the neighborhood. If he didn't get any action, he might move on to the next block.

He'd spent nearly two hours watching the street, but he hadn't seen much of anything. A yard crew had arrived about halfway down the block. One man mowed, another trimmed bushes, while a third plucked a few weeds. They'd packed up and left before an hour passed.

A marmalade cat jumped a backyard fence, sauntered across the street, crossed another lawn, and leapt over another fence.

A dog barked. *Probably not thrilled with the feline visitor.*

A few minute later, a mail carrier drove from one house to another depositing envelopes and packages in the many unusual mailboxes. A couple resembled the house behind them. Several were painted in red, white, and blue patriotic themes. Most were of the regular metal variety, some mounted on wooden posts. Others sat on rock or brick stands. Doug bet they cost far more than any of the mailboxes in other parts of Rocky Bluff.

The first passenger car, a fairly new black Jeep, passed him with two young men inside, possibly in their late teens. He watched the Jeep go all the way to the corner and turn left.

A thought struck him. *Kids aren't in school now and have plenty of time to see what their neighbors are doing.* Right when he started his car, his phone rang. It was Beth.

"What's wrong?"

"Nothing, Dad, except what was wrong when you left."

"Why are you calling?"

"Kayla and I've been talking about your case."

"Aren't you supposed to be doing your schoolwork?"

"We're taking care of it. Listen, Dad, we have an idea who might be doing the garage burglaries."

Doug kept driving while he spoke to his daughter. He followed the Jeep around the corner and continued as it headed down the road that led back to town. He felt conflicted because he might be missing some action going on in another part of the neighborhood.

"Don't you want to hear what we're thinking?"

"Of course, I do. Go ahead."

"It's probably a high school kid. Everyone is home now doing their schoolwork on Zoom."

"Good thought." Maybe they were right.

"Not only that, Dad, there's a senior who's been advertising golf clubs and tools on eBay and a high school group on Facebook."

"Do you think you could find it again when I come home?"

She laughed. "Of course."

"Does the seller identify himself in eBay?"

"No, that's not how it works. And on Facebook he's using a phony name."

The Jeep sped up as it made the last turn into town.

As Doug, followed, the gray fog rose up to greet him. "I think you've got something, but right now I'm following possible suspects. Falls into the category you've mentioned."

"High school kids?" Beth asked.

"Don't know for sure, but they look the right age. Got to go." Right before he disconnected, he heard his daughter cheer.

What happened next couldn't have been more perfect.

The Jeep drove all the way down to the alley that ran behind Valley Boulevard and entered. Doug didn't follow, but he stopped where he could see part way down the alley. The Jeep pulled into the parking lot Doug knew was behind the law firm of Jacobian, Kadish, and Associates.

He debated whether or not to get out of his car so he could see what the pair in the Jeep were up to. But he was glad he hadn't when the Jeep backed up and came roaring out of the alley.

The driver kept the speed about five miles above the limit, and headed back up the road to the neighborhood on the bluff. Though Doug doubted either the driver or the passenger had noticed him, he slowed down but kept the vehicle in sight.

The Jeep passed the place where he'd first spotted them. It turned in at the next street. Doug continued on and went around the block. He only pulled out far enough to see what was going on.

The Jeep had backed into the driveway of a garage in the middle of the block. The large one-story brick house sprawled over what must've been a quarter of an acre. From what he could see from his viewing spot, the home was definitely the biggest in this part of the neighborhood.

As he watched, the driver and the passenger climbed out of the car, and the garage door slowly opened. The two young men disappeared into the interior.

Doug punched the number for Lizette Butler.

She answered immediately. "What's going on, Milligan?"

"I'm on the bluff in the 240 block of Encinitas Ave. I'm confident I'm watching your garage burglars in action. Get up here as quick as you can and make your arrest." It pained him not to be able to jump out of his SUV and nab the suspects.

"Great news. We're not too far away. I've been showing Officer O'Brien what's on the other side of the freeway. We're on our way."

Though he probably didn't need to tell her, he said, "Don't use your siren. You don't want to scare them off." Doug watched the two young men carry toolboxes, car accessories, large cardboard boxes, a cooler, and other items from the garage and put them in the Jeep.

He feared they might finish before Butler and O'Brien arrived. If necessary, Doug was prepared to follow them wherever they went, but he'd promised Chief Taylor he wouldn't make physical contact with anyone.

Chapter 18

As promised, Lizette and her trainee arrived in their patrol car with lights flashing.

When they passed, Doug gave them a thumbs up.

With screeching brakes, they parked right behind the suspects' Jeep. One of the young men, tall with longish light hair, dropped the box he was carrying and ran for his vehicle. When he realized the cop car blocked his in, he raced off down the block.

The other guy stood at the back of the Jeep, not moving. His mouth gaped open.

Lizette's trainee jumped from the passenger side of their car and lunged after the runner, while she approached the fellow who seemed frozen to his spot.

Doug leaned out his open window so he could hear.

She ordered him to put his hands on the back of the Jeep and patted him down. He didn't speak. Smaller than the first suspect, this one wore a sweatshirt with a hoodie pulled up over his head.

The trainee, O'Brien, had caught the runner and marched him to where Lizette had handcuffed her suspect. Doug watched as they walked the two young men to the curb and had them sit down.

Lizette approached Doug's car, but she stayed a few feet away. "Neither of these young men has any ID on them, but they have cellphones, which we've confiscated. Won't be long before we've identified them. I've bagged the garage opener they used. What I wonder is do you know who this house belongs to?"

"Not exactly, but it'll be easy enough to find out."

"I know I can do an Internet search."

"Easier still, the victim of this burglary is either a lawyer at the law office of Jacobian, Kadish, and Associates, or one of their clients. It's where those two yayhoos filched the garage door opener. I suspect it happened the same way your partner described." He paused for a moment. "I'll give the law office a call and see if I can find out for you."

"That'd be great. We're going to need the owner to come and identify the items loaded in the Jeep."

"I'll contact the office now and explain the situation. Someone will probably respond quickly." Doug made the call.

Once he'd described the situation to the person who answered the phone, she immediately connected him to the attorney named Kadish.

"What's going on, Detective Milligan?"

"Do you live on Encinitas Avenue on the bluffs?"

"Yes."

"Your garage was burglarized, and the suspects have been apprehended."

"How can that be?"

"They stole your garage door opened out of your car."

"My car is sitting here in the parking lot."

"I know, but your garage door opener is no longer in it."

A moment of silence. "I'll come home immediately."

Doug signaled to Lizette, and she came over to his car, still maintaining her distance. "Attorney Kadish is coming home. Why don't you call for another officer to come get your suspects and take them in. You'll be busy for a while taking fingerprints and photos and making an inventory of the stolen items. Once the Jeep is unloaded, have it towed to the storage yard."

She nodded and grinned, though Doug suspected she already knew what needed to be done.

"Thanks for your help, Milligan."

"My pleasure. Lots better than sitting at home doing nothing." He knew Stacey could probably think of some jobs for him. Since she couldn't go to work either, he'd better join her. She'd probably like to hear about how the burglary investigation turned out.

~~~

A knock came on Chief Taylor's door. She wasn't expecting anyone, so something must've happened. "Come in."

Ryan Strickland stepped inside. As always, sharp-looking in his uniform, with silver strands sprinkled through his short-cropped hair. "Afternoon, chief."

"Afternoon. What brings you here? Not bad news, I hope." All she needed was to have another man out, a possibility since both the Milligans had been exposed to the virus.

"Not sure yet. Our computer expert has been monitoring several sites hinting at a plan of targeting a small beach town on the coast for a big demonstration."

"What kind of demonstration?"

"A protest against the president, the police, and a potpourri of dislikes and discontent."

"Is it supposed to be peaceful?"

"Aren't they all supposed to be peaceful? But when you get a big bunch of people together, it's like rubbing two matches together. Something always triggers a flare-up."

Taylor agreed. "Have they given any indication of their target area?"

"Not exactly, but some indication is it might be between Oxnard and Santa Barbara. I suppose some might consider Oxnard and Ventura small, but we're definitely the smallest of the beach towns around here."

"Any day or time mentioned?"

"Not yet. Right now, they are recruiting people to join in."

"Let me know as soon as you find out anything more."

"Of course." Strickland made a near-military turn and left.

This news couldn't have come at a worse time. The department was so shorthanded, plus in the next few days, who knew how many of her officers might show symptoms of the virus?

She picked up the phone and called Devon.

He answered quickly. "Chandra? You aren't backing out on our dinner tonight, are you?"

"No, no, nothing like that. I do have some bad news, though."

"Oh, no. I'm certainly getting tired of bad news."

"We're hearing about a protest being planned in a place that sounds too much like Rocky Bluff."

"Do you know when?"

"Not yet. But the problem is, as we both know, we don't have enough manpower to protect our city."

"I've been thinking about what we could do in a case like this. Surely you could call on neighboring law enforcement."

"Yes, but I'd like to have protection already within our city limits, and right now, that seems to be impossible."

"I've got a couple of the council members here in my office right now. We'll discuss the problem. Maybe someone will come up with an idea."

She doubted they would. Most of the council members seemed focused on saving money, not what was best for the town. She tried to sound enthusiastic. "Good. You can tell me all about it tonight."

"I'm looking forward to spending more time with you."

"Me, too." And she was, but she was also glad they were meeting at her house.

Chapter 19

After making all her phone calls, Stacey retreated to her bedroom to say her own prayers for her mother. She had no idea how Clara had come in contact with the virus. Because she and her dad had cared for Davey during the day, she'd taken extra care not to expose herself to others.

She decided to call her dad and find out how he was feeling and if he knew how they'd been exposed.

His first words were, "Have you heard from your mother, honey?"

"Yes. She's asked for prayers from everyone." Stacey swallowed. "She doesn't want to be put on a ventilator."

"She told me that, too, but unless she improves, it will happen whether she wants it or not."

"Dad, she said she'd rather die." Tears stung Stacey's eyes.

"I know, honey. We'll have to trust in the Lord."

She sighed. "Dad, do you know how you two were exposed? I thought you were being careful."

"You know your mom. We heard one of her friends who lives alone was sick, and she insisted we take her some food. We went together. What was supposed to be a case of the flu turned out to be the virus. Her friend didn't let us know right away. When your mom and I started feeling bad, we called you to come get Davey. We both went in for testing. Neither of us thought we could possibly have the virus, but we were wrong."

Stacey fought to keep from crying. "I don't want to lose either of you."

Her dad chuckled. "I don't want you to, either. How are Davey and the girls?"

"We're all fine. Is there any way you can get in to see Mom?"

"No, but as long as she's able, she'll stay in contact with me by her phone. She can't ever talk long because she doesn't have her charger with her."

And Stacey knew her mother couldn't talk at all if they put her on the ventilator. "I wish there was more we could do."

"Keep on praying. I love you, honey. Take good care of your family." He disconnected.

Stacey's parents, Clyde and Clara, had been married for a long, long time. Despite her father's upbeat attitude, she knew he was as worried as she was, probably more.

~~~

It was evening before Doug heard from Felix Zachary.

His first words were, "I had an interesting afternoon. The real estate lady gave me Roger Endicott's new address, and it's way up in the hills above Santa Barbara."

"Did you go there?"

"Yes, though the chief wasn't thrilled. Told me to take a quick look and get back as soon as possible. We've got two more guys out sick. I may be going on patrol duty soon."

"Bummer. Wish I could come back on duty."

"Wish you could, too. Anyway, Endicott's new home is in an area off the San Marcos Pass. Sometime you'll have to go up there. It's a beautiful drive."

"So, what did you find out?"

"Not a whole lot except Endicott must have plenty of money. His new place is a huge log-cabin-style home with an attached garage. There are neighbors, but they're situated far enough apart and surrounded by enough trees that even if they wanted to, they couldn't keep track of one another."

"Were you able to make contact with him?"

"Rang the bell and knocked. He either wasn't home or didn't want to talk to me."

"Any sign of the missing woman's car?"

"No, but it could be in the garage. I got out and looked in the one window on the side but it's covered with something, so I couldn't see in."

"What about Endicott's car?"

"I didn't see it. Might have been in the garage or he wasn't home. There wasn't another vehicle on the premises where I could see it. In better times, I'd put someone up there to keep an eye on the place. It's not possible right now."

Doug smiled. "I could do it. I helped out with a case today doing surveillance." He explained to Felix about the garage burglary.

"The chief was good with it?"

"Yes, as long as I didn't make physical contact with anyone."

"See what she says about doing it again. Of course, we have no way of knowing whether this guy even has Geneva Portman, but it's the only lead we've got."

"I'll run it by her and see what she says."

"That would be great."

"Any news about the victims of the house fire?"

"Not yet."

~~~

When Doug got home, he found everyone gathered in the kitchen. It looked like they were making enchiladas, two kinds. Stacey loaded flour tortillas with pieces of cooked chicken, onions, shredded cheddar cheese, and chopped green chilis. Beth and Kayla sprinkled cheese on another casserole of rolled corn tortillas already covered with a green enchilada sauce. Doug knew those enchiladas were minus the chicken.

"Great, you're home." Stacey wiped her hands on a tea towel. She gave him a big hug and a kiss. "Dinner will be ready shortly. Once we get the enchiladas in the oven, it'll only be a half an hour or less."

"Did you catch the guys who broke into the garage?" Kayla asked.

"We did. Of course, I didn't do any of the arresting, but we caught them right in the act."

Beth slid the dish they'd been working on into the oven. "Was it kids from school like we thought?"

"I don't know the identities of the suspects, but they certainly looked the right age. I'll call Lizette Butler tomorrow and ask."

Stacey had finished with her larger casserole of enchiladas and poured a red sauce over it. "Davey, do you want to put some more cheese on top?"

He grinned and got on his knees on his chair and got busy. Every so often, he popped a finger full of cheese into his mouth.

"How did things go around here today?" Doug got a beer out of the refrigerator, opened it, and took a long swig.

"Everyone was busy with their schoolwork. The girls gave Davey a hand when he got stuck with his Zoom meeting. I did some laundry and baked a cake." Stacey pointed out the chocolate cake in the middle of the kitchen table. "I thought we should eat in the dining room tonight."

"Are we celebrating something?"

"No. I wanted to do something different. I've been so worried about my mother. I'm trying to keep busy."

"Any news?"

"No. Talked to my dad. He seems to be doing all right. At least, he didn't complain about feeling too bad. He's worried about Mom, too, I know, but he sounds okay."

Davey finished sprinkling the cheese and stared at his mother. He asked again, "Is Grandma going to die? I don't want her to die."

"None of us do. A lot of people are praying for her."

"I've been praying, too."

She put the casserole dish in the oven next to the other one.

"Good for you, Davey." She pulled plates from the cupboard. "Let's set the table in the dining room."

Doug knew she didn't want to discuss her mother's condition anymore. He guessed she had a hard time to keep from crying. "I'll take the glasses in."

Beth and Kayla grabbed the silverware from the drawer.

He was anxious to give Chief Taylor a call and ask for permission to do surveillance at Endicott's house, but it could wait until after dinner.

~~~

Chandra Taylor took a quick shower and decided to dress more casually than usual. She chose a simple cotton sundress, one that was comfortable but fit her well. She slipped into a pair of sandals.

Because Devon was providing the dinner, she decided to set the table in the kitchen with her favorite set of dishes, the ones with varied shades of blue. Though she thought about making margaritas to go with the Mexican food Devon was bringing, she decided iced tea was a better choice. She had a pitcher full in the refrigerator, glasses and silverware on the table. She was ready.

Devon showed off his perfect white teeth in a broad smile when she greeted him at the door. Definitely the most handsome and also intelligent man she'd ever dated. Devon had decided to dress more casually, too, and his collared, short-sleeved lime-green polo shirt showed off his muscled biceps and wide shoulders. Tan slacks covered his slim hips and legs.

Delicious smells emanated from the large bag he offered her.

"Come in, come in." She led the way to the kitchen. When she set the food on the counter, Devon slipped his arms around her and turned her to face him.

"I've been thinking about doing this all day." He embraced her and gave her a long, sensuous kiss.

Of course, he'd kissed her before, but there was something new and a bit unsettling about this one.

"Oh, my, you surprised me."

"A welcome surprise, I hope."

Chandra felt her cheeks warm. Not knowing how to answer, she turned back to the food and began setting it on the table. "This looks wonderful, Devon. I'm so glad you thought of it. I don't know about you, but I'm starving."

His lips turned up slightly. He seemed amused by her discomfort. "We need to take more time to be together."

"It's not easy with the jobs we have."

She passed him a plate with tacos, rice, and beans and kept one for herself. Why, oh why, did she feel so uncomfortable? Was it because this was the first time he'd been inside her home?

"It's time we both made more time for our private lives." He took a bite. "They gave us both kinds of salsa. I didn't know if you liked the hotter kind or not." He pointed to the two small plastic tubs on the table.

"I like the spicier one."

They continued to make conversation through their meal. Chandra told him about the two officers who'd been exposed to the virus. "With Detective Milligan and his wife out, and now two more, we barely have enough coverage."

"That's not good, is it? Especially with the threat of outside protestors coming here."

"I'm not against protestors if they would stay peaceful, but that seldom happens. One good thing we have going for us is our citizenry has shown no unusual animosity toward the police."

"But the fact still stands. You don't have enough manpower in case of trouble."

"No, we don't."

"The council discussed the problem. One thing we came up with is perhaps you could use the fire department to help back you up."

"There aren't many of them either, and they aren't armed."

"They do have big fire trucks and water hoses."

"Ah, I see what you're thinking."

"Don't forget about the volunteer firefighters, I bet they'd want to help too."

She thought for a moment, and a plan began to develop. "I'll run this idea by the fire captain tomorrow and see what he thinks."

The topic changed to Kayla. "How is your daughter doing being separated from you?"

"Frankly, I don't think it bothers her at all. I know she cares about me, but we don't really have a close father-daughter relationship."

"Give it time. It will happen."

"Right now, she seems quite content to be staying with the Milligans. Of course, I wasn't thrilled that the

Milligans let her and their daughter go off to the beach like that. It could have been disastrous."

"I can understand them wanting to get out of the house. And of course, now with the situation with the Milligans, Kayla along with their family, have to wait it out to make sure they haven't contracted the virus."

"That worries me, too. If she'd been home, she wouldn't have been exposed."

"But if she'd have been home alone all day, she would certainly have complained and probably driven you nuts."

"You're right. I know she's much happier being able to hang out with Beth and the rest of her family."

"The Milligans are good people. Even though Detective Milligan is off work for the next few days, he managed to help capture a couple of young thieves." She explained what had happened.

Once they'd finished eating and cleaned up the kitchen, Devon said, "The big reason I wanted to spend more time with you, Chandra, is I think it's time we upped the level of our relationship."

That unsettling feeling Chandra had experienced earlier returned. "In what way?"

"From friendship to something more meaningful."

Chapter 20

Despite having to finish up the investigation, turning in the fingerprints they'd taken, and writing reports, something the detectives would have done in normal times, Lizette made it home before Gordon had to leave. He'd obviously eaten a dinner of leftovers, something they both often did if there was no time to cook. She always made big dinners so there would be leftovers.

Though it hadn't happened when she first started on the police department, it didn't take long before she'd realized Gordon had all the attributes she'd always wanted in a man. When he saved her life during a dangerous situation, she knew he was brave as well as being good-looking. He was one of the most honest and ethical people she'd ever met. His open personality had won her over. She hadn't hesitated a moment when he proposed.

He greeted her with a kiss. "You look a bit frazzled. Busy day?"

"It was indeed. Patrick and I caught two burglars in the act. It was at least their second time around. We had a lot of help from Detective Milligan."

Gordon tilted his head and raised his eyebrows. "I thought Doug was quarantined because of the virus."

"He is, but Chief Taylor didn't want us off patrol for so long, and she gave him permission to do our surveillance."

"That's wild."

"Worked out perfectly." She filled him on the details of the case.

When she'd finished and answered all of her husband's questions, she made a face. "And not good news: two more of our guys out were notified they've been exposed to the virus."

"As if we weren't shorthanded already. Sounds like your trainee is working out."

"He's great. Because of our limited manpower, the chief wants Patrick working on his own tomorrow."

"Is he ready?" Gordon asked.

She shrugged. "Ready or not, it's going to happen. We don't have enough on duty, and we need the coverage."

"I hope things lighten up soon."

"Doesn't look like it. There's a rumor going around that we may be hit by a bunch of protestors soon."

~~~

When Doug called Chief Taylor, he knew he'd interrupted something. She sounded a bit breathless when she answered.

"Yes, detective."

He explained what Felix Navarro had found out about Roger Endicott.

"Who is he?"

It wasn't like the chief not to remember details about a case. "The man who our missing woman, Geneva Portman, once had an affair with. One of her friends mentioned Mrs. Portman had seen him recently."

"Yes, yes, I remember now. So, what is it you want me to know?"

"Because the department is so short-handed, Felix can't do surveillance on Endicott's new residence, but I could."

"Do either of you have any reason to believe Endicott might have or know anything about Mrs. Portman's whereabouts?"

"No, not really, but we don't have any other leads. If she'd had an accident in that fancy car of hers, we'd certainly have been notified by now."

"It's your time. Do as you see fit. Remember, though, no physical contact." She hung up.

Odd, she usually had more interest in anything to do with a case. Not this time though. She's seemed anxious to get back to whatever he'd interrupted.

~~~

Doug was up and dressed before Stacey came into the kitchen. None of the kids had made an appearance.

"You look like you're ready to go."

"I am. I made a lunch and a thermos of coffee."

"You're going to leave without eating breakfast?"

"I'll pick something up at a drive-through."

Though they'd discussed his plan for today, he could tell Stacey wasn't happy about it.

"Don't you think it's a bit risky doing surveillance so far from Rocky Bluff? You can't confront your suspect or even make an arrest."

"I'm going to observe. Hopefully find out if there's any reason to suspect this man had anything to do with Mrs. Portman's disappearance."

"I'm surprised the chief is letting you do this since you don't have any evidence against this guy."

"Honey, he's our only lead. If Mrs. Portman had an accident in her car we'd have word by now. The only lead we've had is about the affair she had years ago with this Endicott fellow and the fact she'd seen him recently."

"It's such a long shot. I think you'll be wasting your time."

"You're the one who told us her friend said the missing woman had seen Endicott in Rocky Bluff and he'd made her feel uncomfortable."

"Not much to go on."

"Something is better than nothing. It's all we've got right now."

~~~

Doug drove up San Marcos Pass and felt a tad guilty. Yes, his destination was part of his job, but he felt guilty about being so happy he didn't have to stay home. The drive itself was beautiful. He'd decided to use the SUV rather than the VW so he'd have some power in case he needed it. If he had to do a chase on mountains roads, the VW would be inadequate. The mere thought of a possible chase gave him a shot of adrenalin.

Yes, he felt sorry for Stacey having to remain home, but she needed to be there in case there was any news about her mother. Stacey would be devastated if she lost her mom. Closer than most mothers and daughters, they acted like friends. When Doug first met Stacey, she and Davey had lived with her parents since she'd been widowed. Stacey still turned to her mom in times of crisis, or when she merely wanted a female to talk with.

There wasn't anything Doug could to do about his mother-in-law's situation. Time to turn his thoughts to what he was going to do when he arrived at Endicott's place. He'd have to find somewhere to park the SUV where he could keep an eye on the house but would be hidden from view.

The higher the altitude, the prettier the surroundings. Doug knew scant about the area other than the first to live here were the Chumash Indians. He could see why others had decided to settle in the foothills and higher altitudes. Oak, spruce, and other trees sprouted up through the thick, green underbrush.

He located the road he needed to turn on to reach Endicott's new residence. Though the surface was asphalted, the road itself so narrow, Doug hoped he wouldn't meet another car. It would be a tight squeeze. He drove past clusters of mailboxes and lanes that split off from the road. Vegetation hid any view of homes.

He spotted another break in the foliage off to the right with a small white sign with the name of the street he sought—Viewpoint. The gravel lane wound this way and that, through the trees and breaks with small signs with numbers at intervals, but he seldom caught a glimpse of a house. Once, he spotted a red tile roof poking through the oak trees.

Finally, he came to the number he sought. He turned onto a carved spot in the hillside, a driveway that made a sharp curve then opened up to a large log-cabin-style home with an attached garage, exactly as Felix Zachary had described. Though many trees, oaks and pines, surrounded the sides, the back seemed to be cleared off more. Doug guessed it gave the rear of the house the promised view of the city below and perhaps even the ocean.

Now, the problem was where to park so he could watch but not be seen. He gazed all around, but couldn't see anywhere he could hide his big SUV. He backed away from the house, hoping the occupant hadn't noticed him, and headed farther up the behind Endicott's place and no doubt toward another residence.

Not sure what he should do, he continued until he came to a house with a colonial look. Columns supported a wide upper-story balcony and a portico on the roof, facing west. The grounds had been cleared, and an immaculate lawn surrounded it. Good for fire protection, Doug supposed, but it seemed out of place.

He made a U-turn and drove slowly toward Endicott's place. Before he reached it, he spotted a bit of space under a sprawling oak tree. He backed in, wondering if he'd have enough of a view of the front of Endicott's house if he parked. Only way to find out was to do it.

The branches of the oak scraped the top of his vehicle. He stopped inches short of the broad trunk. Hopefully, he'd be hidden enough not to be noticed by Endicott or his neighbors.

Doug peered through the windshield. Perfect view of the garage and the doorway. He guessed, by the set-up of the house, the front faced the view, and the part he could see was the back. Since that's where the garage was, it was probably the most important to him.

Chapter 21

Stacey's anxiety level had risen to such a high level, the minute Doug stepped out of the house, she used the landline, dialed the hospital, and asked for Maria.

She waited a long time and began to wonder if the person who'd answered had forgotten she was waiting.

Finally, Maria's voice came on the line. "Nurse Navarro, how may I be of help?"

"Oh, thank goodness. Maria, it's Stacey. Can you check on my mother? I'm going crazy with worry."

"Oh, hi, Stacey. I only got in to work a few minutes ago. I have to check in before I can find out anything for you."

Disappointed, Stacey only managed a squeaky, "Oh."

"We're really busy around here, but I promise, as soon as possible, I'll find out what I can about your mom."

Maria disconnected before Stacey could thank her.

All three of the kids appeared at the same time.

"I'm hungry." Davey, still in pajamas plopped down at the kitchen table.

Both of the girls were dressed. Beth wore black leggings and a bulky bright pink sweater that covered her hips. Matching pink ribbons had been braided into her hair. Kayla's choice: faded jeans and a lavender sweater vest over a long-sleeved white blouse with the tails hanging below the hem of the vest. A purple headband ran through her blonde curls.

Stacey poured herself a cup of coffee. "You're both so dressed up. You know you can't go anywhere."

Stacey pouted. "Oh, Mom, we know. But you do realize when we're doing classroom work on Zoom people can see us, right?"

Kayla laughed. "Some of the kids wear sweats or are still in their pajamas and don't bother combing their hair. That just isn't us."

"No, I can see it isn't." She brought three different kinds of cereal out of the cupboard and set them on the table. "This okay for breakfast? We've still got strawberries you can put on top."

"I'll get the milk." Kayla opened the refrigerator and got out the milk and the bowl of fruit.

"Where's Dad?" Beth put three bowls on the table.

"He's doing surveillance again today."

"Another burglary?" Beth put a scoop of strawberries on her granola.

"Not this time. He's working on the case of the missing woman."

"Did someone kidnap her, and your husband knows where she is?" Kayla fixed her cereal.

"Not really. He and his partner are merely following a lead, hoping it will pay off." Stacey didn't feel the least bit hungry. Davey had chosen cereal with bits of marshmallows and piled on the strawberries.

"Have you heard anything about your mom this morning?" Beth asked.

"Not yet, but hope to soon." Though anxious for news, Stacey also feared what it might be.

~~~

Lizette Butler only spoke to Patrick O'Brien for a moment after the morning briefing. "This is a big day for you, Patrick. You're on your own. Don't hesitate to call me on my cell if you have any questions."

"Don't worry. I will. Thanks for all your help." His big grin, perfect posture, and positive attitude let Lizette know he was anxious for his first day alone to begin.

"You'll do great." Certainly better than the last trainee. The fact that Patrick, besides his academy training, had experience as well as a family gave Lizette assurance all would go well with him.

Both of them headed out to their awaiting cars. She and Patrick would be the only officers on patrol this morning. Hopefully, the day would be peaceful. The weather report stated the fog would lift by noon and the temperatures reach the high seventies. The only problem she could foresee might be too many people taking advantage of the weather and possibly doing things they shouldn't.

~~~

The girls had taken over the dining room table to do their Zoom classes. Books and papers spread across the round top. Davey concentrated on his iPad at the kitchen table. Stacey kept an eye on him while preparing vegetables for soup she planned to serve for supper along with homemade dumplings.

An hour passed before the phone rang. She dropped her knife into the sink and ran for the phone in its cradle at the end of the kitchen counter. Maria Navarro calling.

"Hi, Maria."

"I have news for you."

Stacey breathed deeply. "Good news, I hope."

"Yes, it is. Your mother is doing much better. She didn't have to be put on a ventilator, but she has to stay in the hospital at least one more day. If she continues to do well, the plan is to send her home to recuperate."

"Oh, hooray. Thanks for letting me know."

"Give your father a call, too. We'll let him know tomorrow if he can come get her." Maria paused for a moment. "We've never seen anyone improve quite like your mother has. Everyone's talking about it."

"It was prayer, Maria. She asked me to tell everyone she knew to pray for her. I made many calls, and the people I contacted called others."

"I'm happy for you and your family. Your mother was really sick. A turnaround like she had is like a miracle."

"It was a miracle. Thank you, thank you, Maria."

When Stacey hung up, she squealed.

Davey's eyes opened wide. "Mom, what is it? Everyone in my class can hear you."

She grabbed him and squeezed. "Your grandma is going to be okay."

The girls dashed in from the other room.

"What happened?" Beth took hold of Stacey's shoulders. "Is Grandma all right?"

Kayla was right behind her.

Stacey hugged both of the girls. "Yes, she's doing well, and might even be able to come home soon. All those prayers worked."

She tried to contact Doug, but the call didn't go through.

~~~

Doug found out there was no service where he'd stationed himself when he tried to call Felix to let him know he was near Roger Endicott's place. Not being able to use his cellphone could be a big problem. He wouldn't be able to call for help if he needed it, and no matter what happened, he'd been given orders by Chief Taylor not to physically confront anyone.

Might not be a problem. He'd seen absolutely no movement around the house. Made him wonder if Endicott was home. Maybe it would be a good time to go peek in the windows, see if he could spot something to let him know whether or not Geneva Portman was being held captive.

The thought struck him that perhaps the woman had gone willingly with Endicott. If she wasn't with him, then they had no idea at all where to find her.

He'd drunk nearly all his coffee and needed to relieve himself. Good a time as any to take care of that problem and make his way down toward the house.

His car was surrounded by tall bushes, including some manzanita. He didn't want to be exposed by walking down the lane, so he carefully made his way down the incline through the underbrush. Branches, some with sharp ends, snagged his clothes. A couple of times, he slid on the thick layer of leaves, barely catching his balance.

When he reached solid ground, he paused. He started to walk toward the house when he heard the garage door opening. *Crap, here I stand out in the open.* He scooted to the side and dropped flat.

The vehicle they'd found registered to Endicott, a new Toyota, eased from the garage. The driver, whom Doug recognized as Endicott from his driver's license photo, didn't glance in Doug's direction. *Thank heavens.*

Before the garage door shut again, Doug spotted the front end of a red car. He didn't see enough of it to be sure, but in his gut, he thought it had to be the one that belonged to the Portman woman. If her car was here, no doubt she was, too. Doug hadn't seen a passenger with Endicott, which meant Mrs. Portman probably was in the house, either because she wanted to be or she was being held against her will.

He needed to find out before Endicott returned.

Chapter 22

Since there were only two officers available for patrol, Felix Zachary donned his uniform, signed in for a regulation police car, and covered two patrol areas. Not many vehicles were on the street, but he did give out two speeding tickets and one fix-it citation.

While he was driving, he received a call on his cell from the medical examiner's office. *Finally.*

"What we've learned is the older female and the two children died before the explosion. The explosion and fire killed the older male and the baby. With what little is left of the remains, we're only speculating about what killed the first three victims. There are definite knife marks on the skeleton of the female victim. Our guess is she was killed first. We didn't find any such wounds on what was left of the older children so we don't know the cause of their deaths."

"Thank you."

"We'll be sending you copies of the complete autopsy reports once we're finished with them."

Felix's best guess was Jim Barberick killed his wife and two older children. From where they'd found his and the baby's bodies, he'd been on his way out when the house exploded. When possible, Felix wanted to talk with Captain Santori and see if their arson investigator and the one from the insurance company knew what caused the explosion. Time to call Milligan and give him the news.

The call didn't go through.

Had something happened to Doug? Did he decide to do more investigating than he should?

Felix fought the urge to take off and find his partner. Doug could take care of himself. But, what if he found himself in a situation where he needed help?

It didn't matter. Chief Taylor would never give him permission to leave now to find out what Doug was doing. Besides, Felix had no way of knowing whether or not Doug needed any help.

Shaking his head in an effort to get rid of those thoughts, he tried Doug's cellphone again. Nothing.

He glanced up right when a white Mustang didn't hesitate as it sailed through an intersection with a red light. He switched on his siren and emergency lights.

~~~

Though it had not been officially announced, word was spreading about the possibility of a group of protestors descending upon Rocky Bluff.

Chief Taylor had told the higher-ranking officers, including the sergeants. Though they'd been cautioned not to discuss what might happen until they had an actual date and time, bits and pieces of information filtered down among the ranks.

Lizette had heard a couple of the men talking about it, and wasn't surprised when Patrick O'Brien gave her a call. "Is it true what I've heard about an organized group of protestors coming to Rocky Bluff?"

She hadn't heard the word "organized" attached to the mention of protestors. "I don't know how true it is. There's been no official announcement. Actually, I don't think there's been any announcement at all."

"Is it merely a rumor?"

"I have no idea."

"What will we do if they come and make trouble? From what I can see, we don't have enough manpower to protect our city."

Patrick was right, but she didn't want to make him unnecessarily worried.

"If it's true, you can be positive Chief Taylor has a plan. She's probably not ready to discuss it with us yet because she doesn't want the information leaked to the public."

~~~

Keeping a secret about something being discussed on the Internet wasn't possible. The first to pick up on the news were the teens of Rocky Bluff, understandable since most of them knew more about surfing the web than their parents. Now that they were all home, they had plenty of time to do it.

Kayla heard first. She had finished her school assignment and started roaming the Internet. "Oh, wow, I wonder if my dad and Chief Taylor know about this."

Beth sat across from Kayla. "What?"

"Take a look." She moved her laptop so Beth could see what she'd been reading.

"Wow." Beth leaned back in her chair. "Mom, you need to see something."

"I'm in the middle of making cookies."

"This is important."

Baking seemed to be the occupation Stacey had chosen to occupy her extra time. She dumped chocolate chips into the batter she'd been stirring.

"Mom, it's really important."

Stacey wiped her hands on a dark dishtowel, leaving white streaks of flour, and entered the dining room where the girls had been studying.

Beth pointed to Kayla's laptop. "Take a look at Kayla's computer."

She bent over and read. "Oh, my goodness. Why on earth would they want to pick on a little town like Rocky Bluff?"

"Because they can, I suppose."

"Am I reading this right? They plan to do this tonight?"

Kayla shrugged. "Looks like it to me."

"This couldn't be happening at a worse time. I need to get in touch with Doug." Stacey started toward the kitchen but stopped. "Kayla, give your dad a call and tell him. After I talk to Doug, I'll get in touch with the chief."

Her call to Doug went directly to voice mail. Had something happened to him? No, he was in the hills above Santa Barbara. *Probably no service.*

Next she contacted Chief Taylor.

"Yes, Milligan."

"Chief, did you know that there's a bunch of protestors planning to come to Rocky Bluff tonight?"

"Tonight? I knew a group planned to come sometime. Where did you get your information that it's tonight?"

"Kayla discovered it online."

"Let me talk to her."

Stacey handed her phone to Kayla.

She read what she'd found to Chief Taylor."

Kayla listened for a moment before handing the phone back to Stacey. "She said, 'Thank you.'"

"Did she say what she planned to do?"

"No. That was it."

"I can't get hold of Doug. He should know what's going on."

"Why don't you give Detective Zachary a call? He might know how you can contact him."

It took a while before Felix Zachary answered.

"Yeah, Stacey, what can I do for you?"

"I've been trying to get hold of Doug, but he's not answering."

"I'm having the same problem."

"Do you think he's in trouble?"

"Naw, probably no service where he is."

"Felix, did you know protestors are headed here tonight?"

"Been hearing rumors, but hadn't heard when they planned to come. Are you sure?"

"The mayor's daughter found the information online and told the chief."

"Thanks. I'd better head back to the station. Don't worry about Doug. He knows how to take care of himself."

Stacey couldn't help but worry. Yes, her husband could take care of himself under normal circumstances, but not being able to make contact with anyone took away a big element of safety.

Chapter 23

Once Doug was positive Endicott was out of sight, he went around the garage toward the house. An overhanging porch sheltered what Doug guessed was the back door. There were no windows in the door or beside it.

He knocked.

He knocked again.

He pressed his ear against the door but heard nothing.

He made his way around the side of the house until he came to a large window set into the logs. Peering inside he saw a neat kitchen. Two cups sat on the counter by the sink. An island with a butcher block top was in the middle of the room. Stainless steel appliances and pine cupboards were on the far wall.

He kept moving along the sidewall. The next window had blinds open enough that he could tell he'd reached the dining room. A newspaper lay open on the table. One chair sat askew, with the others neatly shoved in place. So far, except for the two cups, Doug had seen nothing to indicate anyone else was inside.

He moved along, not coming to any other windows, but when he came to the corner, he was surprised to see a large covered deck with two Adirondack chairs and a fancy barbecue. Floor-to-ceiling windows made up the back wall with a double French door in the middle. Going to the windows, Doug peered into a large living/family room with a stone fireplace on the far wall, and an open door to the side. He guessed it led to a hall and bedrooms.

If Geneva Portman was here, likely she was in one of the bedrooms.

He climbed the steps to the veranda and tried the French doors. Locked. Unless there was something blocking them, he might be able to jimmy them open. What was he thinking? Unless he knew for sure the missing woman was here, he shouldn't do anything of the kind.

Once across the deck, he started around the other side of the house. If Mrs. Portman was here, he hoped she was in an outside room where he would be able to see her.

He passed the area with the stone chimney. Fortunately, the yard close to the house had been cleared. Nothing to impede him.

The first window he came to had curtains pulled across with only a slim sliver to peek through. He could only see a massive bed with an imitation fur coverlet of some sort, but he didn't see anything to suggest Mrs. Portman was inside.

The next room had horizontal blinds open a few inches. Doug guessed this was an office because he could see a computer monitor on a large desk, along with a printer. He doubted this would be a place a kidnapper would keep his victim.

It became apparent that there was only one remaining room. This one had two smaller windows. Hopefully, Endicott would be gone long enough for him to check.

A bit higher than the other windows, Doug stood on tiptoes to peer in.

What had once been a slight breeze had grown into a wind, tossing leaves around.

At first, Doug could see nothing inside the room. Peering into the first window, he spotted a dresser with some of the drawers pulled partially out.

When he moved to the second window, he gasped. There on the bed lay a woman, her back to him, but he knew it had to be Geneva Portman. He tapped on the window.

The woman reacted by scooting into an upright position.

He tapped again.

She turned to stare at him, wide-eyed.

He had no way of knowing whether she was being held against her will or not.

He pulled his wallet from his pocket and put his ID with his badge against the glass pane.

The expression on the woman's face changed. She smiled, and she slid off the bed and came to the window. She shouted, "Help me."

"Can you open the window?"

She shook her head. "It's nailed shut."

"Step back and I'll break the glass." Doug found a good-sized rock and smashed it against the window. It shattered. Most of the glass fell inside.

Mrs. Portman hurried toward the him.

"Wait. Let me get rid of all these shards." Using another rock, he cleared away the rest of the glass. "Is there a chair in the room you can climb up on?"

She brought a straight-back desk chair and clambered on it.

Doug held out his arms. "See if you can climb through the window. I'm going to put my mask on right now." He pulled it out of his pocket and hooked it over his ears.

She managed to put one leg, and then the other, through the opening and leaned toward Doug, arms outstretched.

He moved close enough that she could grab hold of him.

With her arms tightly around his neck, he grasped her shoulders and pulled her through the window. He continued to hold her until her feet were firmly on the ground.

Doug took a good look at her. Though she resembled the photographs he'd seen of her, she appeared distraught and a bit bedraggled.

She glanced from side-to-side. "Where's Roger?"

"He left a while ago."

"We need to hurry. He'll be back. He said he'd never let me go."

"We're going to do that right now. Follow me."

Though he didn't want to outpace Mrs. Portman, he moved along the side of the house and the garage.

When he reached the end, he heard a car approaching. The garage door opened.

Mrs. Portman put her hands on Doug's shoulders. "Oh, no, he's back."

Doug pulled his keys from his pocket. "Take these." He pressed them into her hand. "Climb up that hill and you'll find my SUV. Get inside and lock the doors. If I don't join you right away, drive out and head toward Santa Barbara. Find a police station or anywhere you can report what's going on. Send help."

"I don't want to leave you."

"Go, it might be your only chance."

"He has a gun."

"So do I. Now, move."

She started scrambling up the incline, grabbing onto bushes and low-hanging branches.

The Toyota came into the driveway but didn't enter the garage.

Endicott had either spotted Mrs. Portman or Doug.

The driver's side door of the Toyota opened. Endicott got out. "Hey, what's going on?"

Doug held up his wallet with his badge. "Detective Milligan Rocky Bluff P.D. You are under arrest for holding Mrs. Geneva Portman against her will."

Endicott stepped away from the open door. "Is that what she told you?" He laughed. "She came up her on her own. We've been reunited after many years, and it's been a most romantic interlude."

"Sorry, that's not what she told me." Doug hoped he was right. "Turn around and put your hands on the hood of your car."

"How do I know you're really a police officer? With that mask on, you look more like a crook."

"Why don't we do this the easy way? We'll go down to the station, and you can tell your side of the story." Doug moved closer to Endicott, his hand reaching for his gun in its shoulder holster.

"I don't think so." Endicott moved back toward the Toyota and ducked down behind the open door.

He popped up once, gun in hand, and shot.

Doug ducked.

The bullet struck the side of the garage.

"I'll get you next time."

Crap, the guy was determined.

Doug hadn't heard his own car start up, so there was no hope for outside help any time soon. "Put your weapon down."

Another shot was fired.

Doug dashed around the other side of the Toyota. He didn't want to have to keep exchanging fire with this guy.

Endicott fired another shot. Each time he'd ducked down behind his car door. He wasn't paying attention to Doug's movements.

He reached the rear of the car and inched his way around it.

Endicott still crouched, gun in hand.

Doug ran and leaped toward Endicott. He landed on the man's back.

Endicott collapsed. He dropped the gun.

Doug grabbed it and tossed it away.

"Get off of me." Endicott squirmed.

Doug held him firmly. He fished a pair of plastic restraints from his pocket.

"Stop. You're making a big mistake."

Doug pulled the man's arms behind him and put the restraints on his wrists. "I'm going to stand you up now."

"You're going to be so sorry. I'll sue you for false arrest." He stumbled to his feet.

Finally, Doug heard his car engine.

Instead of the SUV going down the hill, it turned into the driveway.

Geneva peered wide-eyed through the windshield. She came so fast, Doug feared she'd run into the back of the Toyota.

Brakes squealed. The SUV stopped inches from the Toyota's bumper. Gravel and dust flew.

Endicott frowned. "Who is that?"

"Mrs. Portman in my car."

Endicott tried to yank himself from Doug's grasp. "She'll tell you she wanted to be with me."

"We'll see, won't we?" Doug held Endicott firmly.

Geneva climbed from the SUV, but she stood beside it.

"Geneva, my sweet. Let this crazy cop know you wanted to be with me."

"I'll do no such thing." She crossed her arms and stared at Endicott.

"Mrs. Portman, is there a phone in the house?"

"Yes. There's no cellphone reception here."

"Let's go inside then. It's time I let my people know what's going on." He shoved Endicott toward the back door. "When I'm done, Mrs. Portman, I think your husband will be relieved to hear you are okay."

Doug called for assistance from the Santa Barbara P.D. It took a bit of explaining for the person he spoke with to understand what was going on. Once Doug explained several times, they assured him a police unit would arrive to take jurisdiction over the prisoner.

While they waited, Endicott continued his argument to convince Doug Geneva had come with him of her own volition.

They sat in the kitchen. Geneva had taken one of the chairs as far away from Endicott as possible. "He's lying. I did not want to be with him in any way. He tricked me. He told me he'd invited Anthony to his place and wanted me to come there, too. I don't know why I believed him except he sounded so convincing. He had some big story about him meeting my husband accidentally in Rocky Bluff and they hit it off. I should have guessed he was lying. Anthony is nothing like Roger. The whole idea of them being friends is crazy."

"I'm a whole lot more like your husband than you realize."

She leaned forward. "You don't even know him. He's calm and even-tempered, and old-school polite. It takes a lot to upset him."

"He's been plenty upset wondering what happened to you," Doug said.

"I'm so, so sorry. I can hardly wait to make it up to him."

"You'll soon be able to, but you'll have to tell what happened to you to the Santa Barbara police, and then again to our department."

"It's all pretty straightforward. Roger had some strange idea that he and I could pick up right from where we ended years ago. I am not the same woman I was back then, nor is he the same man. I am not attracted to him at all."

"You didn't give us a chance."

"I had no reason to. I love my husband."

Doug had some questions he'd like answered, too. "Why don't you tell me what happened when you first got up here?"

"When I didn't see Anthony's car, I should have left right then, but I didn't. Foolishly, I got out of the car and asked where Anthony was." She glared at Endicott. "He gave me some story about Anthony going to the store to pick up some items for a barbecue. Another red flag. Anthony hardly ever does any shopping. However, I couldn't believe Roger would out-and-out lie. He convinced me to go in the house with him. Right away, I knew I'd made a big mistake. When I told him I was going to leave, he dragged me into the bedroom where you found me. He only let me out to use the bathroom and bring me food. He kept trying to convince me I wanted to be here with him."

"She did want to be here. I knew it wouldn't take much to rekindle what we once had, and she'd thank me.

Anything would be better than being married to that boring old man."

"Times have changed, Roger. You need to take a good look at me. I'm not the wild, racy woman you knew long ago. I'm old and content to spend the rest of my life with dear good and kind Anthony."

"The sparks are still there, Geneva. I can feel them."

"You're delusional. Those sparks fizzled out years ago."

Listening to Mrs. Portman and watching her expressions convinced Doug she spoke the truth. Anxious to get back home, he knew it would be a long while because of how long it would take to explain to the Santa Barbara P.D. what had gone on and why he was involved. They'd no doubt book Roger Endicott because he'd held his prisoner in Santa Barbara county. Mrs. Portman would have to tell her story again before she could go home.

What he wasn't looking forward to was explaining to Chief Taylor why he'd had to make physical contact with so many people.

Chapter 24

Late that afternoon, Felix Zachary visited Captain Santori of the fire department. They met in the captain's small office in the fire station. Felix shared what he'd learned from the medical examiner. "We'll never know exactly what happened, but the ME says the wife and older children died before the fire.

"Makes sense. What it looks like to us is someone, most likely the husband, opened the gas vents with the intention of getting out of the house with the infant before it blew up. He didn't make it. Pilot light from the water heater may have set it off."

"Sad."

The phone rang. Santori answered. He listened, then frowned. "Are you sure?"

"What do you want us to do?"

"We can do. We'll get on it right away." He hung up. "That was Chief Taylor. She wants our help with something that's supposed to happen this evening."

Felix wasn't sure what Santori meant. "Like what?"

"You haven't heard? Supposed to be a bunch of demonstrators headed to our city."

"I heard rumors, but I didn't realize they'd set a day."

"According to your boss, it is definitely this evening."

"I better get back and find out what's going on."

"No doubt I'll see you later on."

~~~

Chief Taylor asked Devon, in his capacity as mayor, to come to the police station to discuss the plan of action for the evening.

He, along with Captain Santori of the Fire Department and as many of her officers she could spare, met in the squad room.

Before everyone arrived, Chandra changed into her uniform. When she stepped in front of those gathered, she took a deep breath and straightened her jacket. "We know a group of protesters plans to invade Rocky Bluff this evening. Because of the behavior of such groups who have visited other cities, we are too understaffed to protect our homes and businesses adequately."

She could tell by the expressions on the faces in front of her, some had heard the rumors while only a few others exhibited surprise. "Mayor Duvall and I have been discussing the best and most practical way to solve this problem." She glanced toward Devon and smiled.

"I've already spoken with the fire department, and they have agreed to help us."

Santori nodded.

Chief Taylor continued, "The best way to protect our city is not to allow anyone in. We will block the freeway entrances and exits. And we will do it in such a way no one can get through. It may cause some inconvenience to some of our citizens who are coming home, but it will be nothing compared to the inconvenience of looters and those who want to destroy homes and businesses. I'm going to outline the plan quickly, and the sergeants will hand out individual assignments."

Santori stood. "I'm on my way to get my people situated."

~~~

It took a while to get through to the Santa Barbara police why he wasn't on official duty.

When they found out he'd been exposed to the virus, everyone who hadn't had on masks quickly donned one. He'd been escorted to a large room where he was left alone.

An hour went by before a sergeant named Conway, who'd no doubt pulled the short straw, entered. A no-nonsense individual, one who'd been around a while, straddled a chair across the room.

"Okay, now tell me why you're the one who was assigned this job since you were supposed to be quarantined at home."

"Our department has been undermanned for a while. Now with COVID, it's gotten worse. We only had one lead as to where Mrs. Portman might be, and no one to follow it up. I volunteered. When our suspect left his house, I figured it was the time to see if I could find her, and I did. There is no cell service there, and I had to do something. I couldn't leave her there."

"No, I guess not." He sighed heavily. "And of course, you had to confront Endicott."

"I had no choice."

"Mrs. Portman has corroborated everything you've told me. We've taken her statement, and one of our officers has taken her home."

Doug knew Mr. Portman would be ecstatic when she arrived. Doug wished he could be there to see the reunion. "I know she's going to be anxious to get her Corvette back."

"We have officers at the Endicott location now gathering evidence. Once we've checked the car, we'll see it's returned to her. We'll contact your department with what we've found."

Conway leaned back in his chair. Of course, you realize that if you do have the virus, you've now exposed

Mrs. Portman, anyone from our department who came in contact with you, and our suspect, Roger Endicott."

"Yes, and I'm sorry, but I feel fine. No temperature, no sore throat, and I can still smell."

"For all our sakes, I hope you keep feeling fine."

"Can I go now?"

"Yes, and I'm glad you were able to rescue Mrs. Portman."

"I am, too."

By the time he left the station, it was dark. He was hungry, but he knew he still had some food he'd brought with him in his SUV.

He wanted to get home and be with his family.

He drove toward Rocky Bluff. When he got close, traffic slowed almost to a crawl. *There must've been an accident.*

As he drew near the exit to Rocky Bluff, he could see all sorts of emergency lights on both sides of the freeway. *Whatever happened must've been huge.*

When he reached the exit, it was blocked by a fire engine and a police car. *What the heck is going on?*

On the other side of the freeway, he spotted more emergency lights, a police car, and some larger vehicles. *Farm equipment?* Cars and vehicles were backed up along the freeway on that side too. Didn't look like he'd be getting home anytime soon. If he could find a good spot to pull off, he'd call home.

~~~

A long line of trucks and passenger cars had been spotted coming from both directions headed toward Rocky Bluff.

Chief Taylor stood beside the fire department's water tender with Mayor Duvall beside her. "We're ready for them."

The men with the tender already had their hose out, ready to use if necessary. The entrance and exits to Rocky Bluff from the north had been effectively blocked, not only by a fire truck but also two police cars and vehicles owned by volunteer firefighters, who stood ready for a confrontation if necessary.

Though she hadn't gone over there, Chandra was in radio contact with Detective Zachary, who was in charge of blocking that entrance from the freeway. "How do things look over there?"

"No one's getting past us. We've got a fire engine, two police cars, and all sorts off big farm equipment, dozers, spray rigs, trucks. No one's getting in. The ranchers and farm owners are all armed." Zachary sounded confident.

"I'm not sure it's such a good idea for folks to have guns. We're not going to war."

"No, but it's lit up enough over here for anyone who thought they wanted to mess with us will have a change of heart."

"Okay. Make sure everyone stays calm."

"Will do."

~~~

When the first of the vehicles reached the two freeway entrances to Rocky Bluff, they turned in, but halted immediately. Both ways were completely blocked.

On Chief Taylor's side, a young white driver leaned out of the driver's side of a black truck. "Hey, what's going on? I need to get through."

Chief Taylor stepped forward. "No strangers are welcome here."

The fireman holding the hose aimed it toward the truck.

"What are you doing?"

"Getting ready to send you on your way." A strong spray of water emphasized the fireman's words

The driver spewed a string of curse words and backed up the truck, barely missing the vehicle behind him. He sped off toward the south.

Devon turned to Chandra. "One down, and who knows how many to go."

A Jeep appeared at the entrance, loaded with young people, probably all in their twenties. They hung out windows and shouted.

"What's going on?"

"Why can't we get in?"

"This is a free country. We have the right to go where we want."

Chandra stood straight. "Not tonight. No one's coming in. Go back where you came from."

The driver revved the Jeep's engine.

The fireman aimed the hose at the Jeep.

Again, a bunch of yelling came from the Jeep.

"What the hell are you doing?"

"You can't do that."

"Hey, don't turn on that hose."

The fireman moved closer.

Another fireman held up part of the hose.

The Jeep backed up and drove back onto the freeway.

The next car came in a short way before pausing and returning to the main highway.

Several more vehicles passed by the entrance moving at a slow rate of speed.

Devon grinned at her. "I think our visitors are getting the message."

"I hope they're passing it on. I don't want to be out here all night."

"How do you think the folks on the other side are doing?"

"I'm not sure, since they don't have a water tender. The threat of being sprayed with a fire hose has been a great deterrent." She keyed in Detective Zachary's cellphone.

"Zachary."

"How's it going over there?"

"So far no one has been brave enough to tackle a bunch of armed and angry ranchers. I don't think the protestors have ever come across such formidable-looking folks. The police cars and uniformed officers haven't made much of an impression, but once they see these grim-faced and armed men sitting on top of their equipment, they're out of here." Zachary's laugh boomed.

"Don't let anyone get trigger happy." Chandra still didn't think having armed civilians was a good idea, but it was working. "If there are any problems, let me know."

"I think we're good. How's it going over on your side?"

"No one wants to get drenched with a fire hose."

"I can see Highway Patrol is starting to pull folks over. Probably giving tickets for obstructing traffic. The excitement may die down soon."

"I hope so, but we'll stay put until we're sure it's over." She turned to Devon. "It's working great, thanks to the ranchers backing up the police."

"I wonder who told them what was going on."

"We've got a most active rumor network. No telling what havoc those protestors might have done on that side of the highway. Those living over there weren't willing to find out."

Chandra planned to stay vigilant until she was sure the protestors had given up.

~ ~ ~

Doug found a place off the shoulder where he could pull over. Vehicle after vehicle passed him, picking up speed as they drove by.

He got out his phone and pushed the button for home.

Stacey answered almost immediately. "Doug, thank goodness. Are you all right?"

"I'm fine, but I don't know when I'll be able to get home. There must've been a major accident at the entrance into Rocky Bluff. Once I finish talking to you, I'll go down to Ventura and come up the other way."

"Don't bother. You won't be able to get in that freeway entrance either."

"What's going on?"

"The police department is blocking protestors from coming into town."

"I'd heard the rumors but had no idea it was happening tonight."

"I've been trying to get hold of you but couldn't get you on your phone."

"I found Geneva Portman. She's probably home by now since she left quite a while before I did."

"That's wonderful. Is she okay?"

"Yes, at least I think so. I had to yank her through a window. Had a bit of a confrontation with her kidnapper, but he's spending the night in the Santa Barbara jail. They'll be the ones prosecuting him since what he did happened in Santa Barbara county." He took a deep breath. "The chief isn't going to be happy with me."

"Why not?"

"I had to come in contact with a lot of people. Mrs. Portman, Endicott, the guy who kept her prisoner, and a bunch of cops from the SBPD."

"Doesn't sound like there was any way you could avoid it."

"She might not feel that way."

"Hey, you rescued Mrs. Portman from her kidnapper."

"And maybe exposed a whole lot of people to the virus while I was at it."

"I'm positive none of us have it. Certainly, none of us has showed any symptoms, and we've been around my folks a lot."

"Speaking of folks, how's your mother doing?"

"Extremely well, and so is my dad. Prayers worked."

He asked about what else was going on and continued to chat with Stacey while waiting for the traffic to get back to normal.

~~~

Gordon Butler and Patrick O'Brien were the only two officers who worked patrol duty and answered calls for assistance in town while everyone else guarded the entrances and exits from the freeway into Rocky Bluff. It was the first time Gordon'd had any interaction with O'Brien, and for being as new as he was, he behaved like a professional. Lizette had done a great job training him.

~~~

Abel Navarro's brother, Mario, reluctantly accepted the fact the COVID-19 virus was a serious threat when one of his employees had to be hospitalized. He didn't stop working, but he wore a mask, and made the two unaffected men do the same. However, he didn't stop grumbling about not being able to see his father.

~~~

The day after the protestors had been thwarted from invading Rocky Bluff, Chief Taylor learned they'd gone on to Ventura where they'd run rampant up and down the streets, broke some shop windows, tried to start fires in businesses, but the Ventura P.D. quickly arrested a few and ran the rest out of town.

~~~

Abel's wife, Maria, worked so many hours at the hospital sometimes she didn't bother to come home. When Abel worked, his other brother's wife took care of Lupita. She promised to follow all the rules Maria spelled out.

~~~

Though at times Ryan Strickland felt his wife, Barbara, might be a tad too zealous when it came to isolating the family, and making him shed his clothes in the garage before coming in to shower, he knew she did it to protect her boys and their daughter. He was willing to do anything to keep his precious Angel safe.

~~~

Doug Milligan finally made it home.

Late the next afternoon, he received a call from Anthony Portman.

"I hope I'm not disturbing you, but I want to thank you so much for rescuing my wife. She told me everything. We are both so grateful. If there's anything we can ever do for you, please ask."

"It was my pleasure, sir." Doug disconnected, feeling good.

When he told Stacey who called, she focused on him intently. "I've been thinking about what you told me about why Mrs. Portman said she went to Endicott's home. Why didn't she call her husband to make sure what Endicott told her was true?"

"That's a good question, but I doubt we'll ever learn the answer."

"You know what I think?"

"What?"

"Let me ask you something first. What did Roger Endicott look like?"

"Not bad for his age. His hair is white, but he has plenty of it. On the handsome side, I suppose. Certainly, in much better shape than Mr. Portman."

Stacey grinned. "I bet Mrs. Portman accepted her old lover's invitation because she was flattered that he was still interested in her after all these years. She might even have wondered if she might have any feelings left for him."

Doug considered what Stacey proposed. "I suppose it's possible, but she didn't give me any indication that was so."

"Of course not. And once she found out he'd lied to get her up there all those thoughts would have disappeared."

The speculations ended because the phone rang again. This time, the ID showed it was Chief Taylor. *Uh, oh, now I'm going to hear about her displeasure because of all the people I came in contact with and potentially exposed to the virus.* He waited a moment before answering. "Detective Milligan."

"Good work yesterday. I read your report."

Surprised, Doug could only think of one thing to say: "Thanks."

He was even more surprised when the chief asked to speak to Kayla.

"One moment."

Kayla and Beth were both in the living room. The TV was on, but they were paying more attention to their iPads.

"Kayla, Chief Taylor wants to speak to you." Doug handed Kayla his phone.

At first as she listened, Kayla opened her eyes wide, then her face exploded into a huge smile. "Thank you. And of course, I will. Hope to see you soon, too."

Still smiling, she handed the phone back to Doug.

"What was that about?" Beth asked.

"Chief Taylor told me my tip about the protestors planning to come last night probably saved the town. She asked me to be sure and let her know if I spot anything else like that on the Internet."

Beth jumped up and hugged Kayla. "You're a hero."

Stacey came in from the kitchen. "It sounds to me like we should celebrate. Dinner's almost ready, and I've got the fixings for hot fudge sundaes."

Davey cheered.

"Sounds perfect to me." Doug moved toward Stacey. "What can we do to help?"

"We'll set the table," Kayla said. "Come on, Beth."

"We've all been working enough. Let's find a good movie to watch tonight." Stacey led the way back to the kitchen.

What a great end to several days of tension. Doug felt proud of his family. Despite living during this difficult time, everyone thrived and managed even to do better than he'd expected. One day they'd look back and realize how they'd become closer and done well despite how crazy the world had become.

The End

About the Author

MARILYN MEREDITH is the author of the Deputy Tempe Crabtree mystery series and the Rocky Bluff P.D. crime series (under the name, F. M. Meredith). She has also written several stand-alone novels, and other books.

She and her husband live in the foothills of the Sierra, much like the place where her heroine, Tempe Crabtree, lives. She once lived in a beach community, which resembles Rocky Bluff.

She loves to hear from readers who have enjoyed her books.

Visit her webpage at http://fictionforyou.com, and follow her blog at https://marilynmeredith.blogspot.com